The Orphan
of
ELLIS ISLAND

The Orphan
of
ELLIS ISLAND

A TIME-TRAVEL ADVENTURE

ELVIRA WOODRUFF

SCHOLASTIC INC.
New York Toronto London Auckland Sydney
Mexico City New Delhi Hong Kong Buenos Aires

ISBN-13: 978-0-590-48246-2
ISBN-10: 0-590-48246-7

Copyright © 1997 by Elvira Woodruff.
All rights reserved. Published by Scholastic Inc.

SCHOLASTIC, APPLE PAPERBACKS, and associated logos are
trademarks and/or registered trademarks of Scholastic Inc.

60 59 58 57 56 55 54 53   20

Printed in the U.S.A.   40

Book design by Kristina Iulo
The text type was set in 14 point Bembo.
The display type was set in Bodoni Poster.
Title Page photograph © Culver Pictures.
The ornament on the chapter openers was used with
permission of the Statue of Liberty National Monument.

First Trade paperback printing, August 2000

ACKNOWLEDGMENTS

To write this story I listened to my family stories and to the stories of many other Italian immigrants. I also visited the museum at Ellis Island. This proved most inspirational, for it was there that I was encouraged to go back in time and to imagine just what an immigrant's journey must have been like. My thanks to the Ellis Island Immigration Museum and to the many fine people who work at preserving this national treasure.

I also wish to thank Barry Moreno and Jeffrey Dosik, Librarians, Ellis Island Immigration Museum, for fact-checking the 'manuscript; Maria Rivera, Director of Training, Administration for Children's Services, for her consultation regarding foster care; and Michelle Patruno, NYU Department of Italian Language and Literature, for reviewing the Italian words. Special thanks also to my editor, Dianne Hess, who smoothed out many a wrinkle, offering just the right glow!

In memory of Francesco and Rose,

and Emma and Giovanni,

and for Elvira Carnicelli,

whose gentle voices led me across

an ocean and back in time.

—E.W.

The Orphan
of
ELLIS ISLAND

CHAPTER ONE

"WELCOME TO ELLIS ISLAND," the ranger from the National Park Service said to the group of fifth-graders standing before her. "This museum is dedicated to the millions of immigrants who passed through these buildings on their way to becoming American citizens."

There was one fifth-grader, however, who was not thinking about the buildings or the millions of immigrants who passed through them. This fifth-grader was thinking about his feet.

If only they would stop growing, Dominic Cantori thought. He stared down at his toes, which were painfully squeezed into a pair of old sneakers. Then he looked around him at all the sneakers on his classmates' feet. Some looked as if they had never been worn before.

Dominic sighed. He longed to a have a new, fashionable pair of sneakers, a pair that fit. But he knew it wasn't going to happen any time soon.

Having new, fashionable sneakers, and keeping up with Dominic's quickly growing feet was almost impossible as long as he lived with one foster family after another.

His feet had grown so much in the past few weeks that he was unable to tie his laces, and he finally just pulled them out.

Whenever he could, when no one was watching, he would slip his feet out of the tight sneakers so that his cramped toes could unbend. He checked now to see that no one was looking, and as the ranger talked on, Dominic silently worked his left heel out of his sneaker.

"As we search our family trees, many of us can find relatives who came through Ellis Island as immigrants," the ranger continued.

Dominic stood for a moment, wiggling his free toes within his sock, wondering about his family tree. What would it look like? He imagined a little twig with one tiny leaf hanging from it. On the leaf was his name. That was it.

Dominic had never known his family. His parents had both died when he was a baby. He had no sisters or brothers. There were no grandmothers, grandfathers, aunts, or uncles. The state had tried to locate any living relatives, but none could be found. Dominic had become a ward of the state, and no one had come to claim him. Now he was living with his third foster family this year, in Brooklyn, New York.

Besides a few possessions that fit into three suitcases, the most important thing that Dominic owned was a gold key that hung from a chain around his neck. You could see that the key was very old. It had been with his mother's belongings when she died.

"It's not real gold," a kid in one of his classes had pointed out, but that didn't matter to Dominic. What mattered were the initials, S.C., scratched on the key. Dominic loved to rub his fingers over them. Sal Cantori had been his father's name, and he was certain the key must have belonged to him.

The key's history, like Dominic's, was a mystery. He had no idea what it was meant to open, but it was the only thing left from his family, something he could touch, something solid. It was his "lucky key" and he wore it always on a chain around his neck. But Dominic wasn't sure just how much his lucky key was working.

In fact, he had been a kid with incredibly bad luck. Dave Santos, his caseworker, had called him just yesterday. Dominic's current foster family regretted to inform him that things weren't going to work out after all. They were moving to California at the end of the month, and they wouldn't be able to take him along. Dave had already begun to look for another family.

Dominic had not been surprised. He had grown accustomed to things "not working out." Even so, the old fear of being abandoned and of having to move in with strangers left his stomach in knots. Once again, Dominic was haunted with the familiar questions. *What would these new people be like? Where would he sleep? Who would he turn to if something went wrong? And how long would he stay there before he was told to pack his things and move on?*

Dominic had been with so many families, that he had developed a game to help him still the fear of having to fit into yet another new place, with strange people, strange noises, and strange smells.

He would lie in his bed at night, whichever bed, in whichever apartment, and as he lay there, he would twist his golden key on its chain, and imagine a perfect family, his dream family. In this family there was always a mother and a father that he would call "Mom" and "Dad."

There would be a refrigerator and cupboards that were always filled with pizza and marshmallows and potato chips that he could have any time he wanted. There would be warm, homemade brownies on the kitchen table when he came home from school. And best of all, in his dream family, there would be brothers to play with and lots of pets to care for. Sometimes he imagined a sheep dog and other times he imagined a parrot or a monkey. In real life Dominic was not allowed to have any pets, because, as his caseworker explained, he never knew if the families he stayed with would allow one.

Unlike in real life, things were perfect in his dream family. And it was this dream family that saw him through the many scary moves and the many long and lonely nights spent under bedspreads that smelled of other people's houses.

Dominic had been in many different schools, in Brooklyn and the Bronx. He had only been at his present school for three days when his new teacher, Mr. Howard, had told him that all the fifth-grade classes would be going on a trip to Ellis Island the following Monday. That had been perfect timing. Dominic loved class trips. He always hoped that each new trip was going to be his best ever.

The soft cadence of the ranger's voice drifted back to him. "Many of you may discover your family history, right here at the Ellis Island museum." But Dominic knew that he wouldn't be one of the "many."

"This is so boring. I wish we could get back on the boat," he heard someone whisper.

Dominic looked in front of him where a red-headed boy wearing fancy, new sneakers whispered to another boy with bristly blond hair. Dominic knew they were best friends, and he also knew the red-haired boy's name was Justin.

He watched as Justin leaned over and burped in his friend's ear. Dominic felt envious as he watched them. He wished that he had a friend who would lean over and burp in his ear. As Dominic imagined himself with such a friend, he giggled out loud.

A boy next to him whispered, "What's so funny?" Immediately, Dominic's smile vanished and he lowered his eyes to the floor to avoid the boy's gaze. The boy shrugged his shoulders and looked away.

Dominic bit down on his lower lip. How he wished he could share his funny thoughts and laugh with someone. But he just didn't know how.

Talking to new kids was always hard for him. And new kids were the only kids he ever seemed to meet.

Dominic hadn't spoken to anyone except the teacher since he arrived. It was the same in every school. He always hoped that he would make a friend, but he never had. He was painfully shy, and was never the one to begin a friendship. And by the time the kids in his class got to know him, Dominic was yanked out of that school and sent off to another.

Justin turned around suddenly and looked at Dominic, then he continued his hushed conversation with his friend. Dominic heard their muffled laughter.

He wondered if the kids were laughing at him. He was used to people making fun of "the new kid." Dave always told him kids did that because they were uncomfortable themselves.

"I know it's hard," Dave often said, "but you've got to let yourself get past 'the new kid' thing. Just be yourself and trust that people will like you."

It always sounded so easy when Dave said that. But learning to trust that people would like him was just one of those things that Dominic didn't think he'd ever be able to do.

Everyone's attention was on the ranger now, as she pointed to a display. Dominic leaned forward and worked his other heel out and wiggled his toes in his sock.

"It was here at Ellis Island that the newly arrived immigrants were questioned and medically inspected to be sure that they could support themselves," the ranger said.

A boy standing beside Dominic leaned over to look at a display and accidentally stepped hard on Dominic's foot. Dominic yelped in pain and surprise. A number of kids turned to look at him and laughed.

"He sounded like a howling dog," someone said.

The ranger continued to speak over the commotion. "Ellis Island has been called 'The Island of Hope' because so many people had hoped to make a new start in America. But it was also called 'The Island of Tears.' Does anyone know why?"

Tears welled up in Dominic's eyes, as a big hand suddenly rested on his shoulder.

Maybe this wasn't going to be the best class trip after all, he thought to himself. As he fingered his lucky key, Dominic turned around and looked up to see his teacher's eyes staring sternly into his.

CHAPTER
TWO

"THIS IS NOT THE TIME to be fooling around, ah . . . ah . . ." Mr. Howard's frown suddenly turned to a look of embarrassment.

Dominic could tell that the teacher had forgotten his name.

"You're making it difficult for the others to pay attention," Mr. Howard finally said. Dominic tried to protest, but the teacher turned his attention back to the group.

Dominic bit his lip and tried hard not to cry, as the class watched him with curiosity.

"Your teachers have told me that you've done research projects on your family histories," the ranger announced in a cheerful voice. "I'd love to hear about some of them."

Dominic suddenly panicked as he watched a flurry of hands go up in the air. He dug his hands into his pockets and began pulling on the little threads that had frayed from the inside seams.

"Why don't you take turns," suggested the ranger. "Each of you can tell me which country your family came from. Let's start with this row first," she said, pointing to a girl beside her.

Dominic's eyes darted anxiously around the group. How on earth was he supposed to answer this? He felt his face grow hot, as the fifth-graders, one after another, proudly named relatives that had come to America from all over the world.

"Poland, Ireland, Russia, Africa," the children called out in turn.

Dominic was filled with anger and shame as he lowered his eyes to the floor.

The secret that he had carried with him wherever he went, from school to school, was about to be uncovered. The idea of revealing the truth that he was alone in the world, abandoned and unwanted, filled him with such dread that he would do anything to keep it hidden.

The sweat gathered on his forehead, as Dominic tried frantically to think of what to say. As the ranger suddenly pointed to him, he reached up and clutched his lucky key with his trembling fingers, and then he opened his mouth to speak.

CHAPTER THREE

"MY GREAT-GRANDFATHER came from Italy," Dominic heard the words come tumbling out of his mouth. He took a gulp of air, anxious to see if anyone would object. No one did. With a wave of relief he had remembered at the last minute how one of his foster fathers thought that the name Cantori was Italian. But without knowing his family history, he couldn't be sure.

Dominic cringed now, as he caught sight of Mr. Howard's wary look. There was something in the way his left eyebrow rose into a crooked arch over his eye.

Dominic filled with embarrassment as he remembered that his teacher had talked to his caseworker. Of course Mr. Howard knew the truth about him. He knew that Dominic didn't know a thing about his family. Dominic swung around to look back at the ranger as she continued her talk.

"To celebrate the many immigrants who risked

so much to come to our country, we have established a special memorial," she announced. "It's called 'The American Immigrant Wall of Honor.' Families and friends of immigrants may have a name placed on the wall for a donation. Do any of you know if you have relatives' names on the wall?"

Dominic watched uneasily as a number of hands went up, including Justin's and his friend's. Dominic threw up his hand. He wanted so much to be like them, to have a family name up on that wall. Mr. Howard's eyebrow arched even higher, and the ranger beamed with delight.

"That's terrific," she cooed, "because we'll all be going to see the wall after lunch. Then we can look for those names together."

"If everyone will follow me," the ranger continued, "we'll move on to the baggage room area." Dominic straggled behind the group as they walked to the center of the room.

Dominic could no longer hear what the ranger was saying. He was too distracted as he stared at the back of Mr. Howard's head. He worried about going to the wall and about how embarrassed he'd be when his classmates discovered that his family name wasn't there.

Why did I have to tell such a big dumb lie? Dominic thought. If only it would all go away.

Dominic couldn't stop worrying as the group

slowly made its way around the museum's first floor, and he hardly noticed the large black-and-white photographs of immigrants that hung on the walls. The sights and sounds of the second floor were lost on him as well. He was unable to concentrate on anything. Even so, the tour went on.

"The telephone receivers you see in the display in front of you are equipped with the taped voices of real immigrants telling their stories," the ranger explained.

Dominic thought of his own story and how he would give anything to change it. He followed the others and mechanically picked up a receiver and listened. The voice of an old Polish woman croaked in his ear. She talked about how dangerous escaping from her country had been.

As she told of the rough, stormy seas and the bad food on the ship, Dominic thought about the ferry ride home. He imagined the jeers and ridicule that would be heaped on him and how his favorite part of the trip, the boat ride past the Statue of Liberty, would be ruined. All the fifth-graders would know the truth about his family, and that he was a liar.

"All right, folks, we're going to the third floor," Mr. Howard called. "Line up at the up escalator, and watch your step."

Dominic hung up the receiver and watched as

the excited huddle of fifth-graders rushed to get in line. He imagined himself standing conspicuously alone. Then the moment Dominic had been dreading would finally arrive. Mr. Howard would announce that it was time to see the wall, the dreaded wall.

As Dominic followed his class to the line by the escalator, he ducked behind one of the display cases, and reemerged in the middle of a group of Japanese tourists who were waiting at the down escalator. He moved along, hidden in the large crowd, and kept his head low as he rode back to the first floor.

Once there, Dominic broke away from the crowd, and ran to the end of the hall. He saw an open door and stepped inside. He smiled at the sight of all the brooms, mops, and bottles of cleaners that filled the little closet. Then he reached for a big flashlight that was sitting on a shelf, clicked it on, and closed the door behind him.

In the glow of the flashlight, Dominic cleared a space in a back corner of the closet, behind some big canvas tarps that were hanging from hooks. When he was sure that he was safely hidden away, Dominic sank down to the floor and took off his sneakers and socks. He turned the flashlight off and wiggled his toes with relief. He welcomed the dark, like a cool, protective black blanket. Now that he was hidden, hidden away from all of them, he could relax.

With a yawn, he laid his head back against the wall and began to wonder what he should do next, but he was too tired to think. All he knew was that he needed to get away.

Dominic yawned again. The strain of the day's excitement was suddenly catching up with him. He found himself struggling to keep his eyes open. But the temptation to give in to the drowsy feeling of sleep was too much for him. Dominic's head drooped onto his chest, as his eyes closed.

I'll take a little rest, he thought. *Just for a few minutes.* Then he thought nothing at all.

CHAPTER FOUR

HIS NECK ACHED. That was the first thing Dominic noticed when he awoke. He lifted his head from his chest. That's when he noticed the second thing. The darkness.

Where am I? he wondered. He stretched out one leg and was startled by a loud bang as his bare foot knocked against a bucket. The noise and the strong odor of disinfectant suddenly brought the memory of the whole dreadful day rushing back to him. Dominic reached down into his lap and turned on the flashlight.

"I wonder if they've gone to the wall yet," he whispered, poking his head out from behind the tarp. He pictured his classmates' accusing faces as they searched for his great-grandfather's name — a name he was certain they'd never find.

"I can't go back with them, and I can't go back to that school," he said grimly. In the glow of the flashlight, Dominic wondered what he ought to do next.

Then he thought of Dave Santos, his case-worker. Dave had promised to find him a new family. Maybe Dave could find him one today.

And a new school to go with it, he thought. *All I have to do is call Dave.* Dominic decided. Then he remembered that he only had his lucky Indian head nickel in his pocket, which wasn't enough money for the phone.

"That's all right," Dominic said to himself with a shrug. "I don't need Dave anyway. I can hop a ferry." His face brightened at this notion, although he didn't take the time to think past what he would do after the ferry ride. It was enough to have a plan that took him that far.

He stood up and made his way across the closet.

That's funny, he thought, as he opened the door a crack. *It's so dark.*

He pushed it open a little further. The bright lights that had been there before had been dimmed. Dominic stepped out of the closet and into the museum. He flicked on the flashlight and took a step to the right. Flashing his light across the huge exhibit hall, he recognized the silver escalator. Gleaming in the darkness, it sat silently, moving neither up nor down. And where were all the people?

What's going on? Dominic thought nervously, taking a few steps forward. By the time he reached the darkened display cases, Dominic's nervousness had turned to fear. There was definitely something wrong, dreadfully wrong. It was all too still, too quiet. Where was everyone? And what had happened to the lights?

Using his flashlight to guide him, Dominic slowly found his way to the entrance doors. He tried the handles, but they were locked. He pressed his face against the glass. To his astonishment, he saw lights twinkling in the distance as boats bobbed up and down over the black waters of the harbor.

"Oh, no!" Dominic gasped, when he realized it was night. He pushed against the heavy door, but it wouldn't budge. He tried opening all the doors again, but they were locked fast. *I must have slept for hours,* he thought.

"Help!" he shouted at the top of his lungs, hoping someone would hear, but his shout only echoed into the eerie stillness. As he bounced his flashlight's beam from one wall to the next, Dominic thought about his classmates, and Mr. Howard, his teacher. Had they gone back to the school without him? Hadn't anyone missed him?

Whether anyone missed him or not, it didn't matter much now, Dominic realized. What mattered was that it was dark, and he was all alone, and hungry, and trapped in this museum until morning.

What am I supposed to do here all night? he thought. "Is anybody here?" he called out. "There's got to be someone else here."

"Hey," he shouted. "Can you hear me? Help!" As he made his way across the room, his shouts for help became more and more desperate. He called on anybody he could think of to help. "Hey, Mr. Night Watchman, help! Hey, Dave, help! Hey, Mr. Howard, help! Hey, Mr. President, help! Hey, anybody, help!"

And finally, when he was sure there was no one around who could hear him, Dominic cried aloud, "I'm scared. I'm really scared."

CHAPTER
FIVE

AFTER TRYING EVERYTHING he could think of to get out of the museum, Dominic walked up the still escalator steps to the second floor. He shone his light up to a huge, black-and-white photograph of an immigrant family that hung on the wall. Dominic stopped to read the words below it. "An Irish family arriving at Ellis Island, 1911" was all the caption said.

Dominic studied the picture. There was a mother, a father, and nine children (he counted them). To his surprise, he realized that they were all boys, at least eight of them were, for he wasn't sure about the baby in the mother's arms. Even so, eight brothers! He whistled out loud.

Dominic had always dreamed of having a brother, but having eight would be like winning the lottery! He stared up at the photograph and imagined himself standing in the long line of fair-haired boys.

Soon Dominic walked from photo to photo, trying on one family after another. He saw himself surrounded with Chinese brothers and sisters in one picture, leaning against a tall Russian father in another, and in the arms of a smiling Gypsy mother in yet another.

He spent a long time roaming the hallways and rooms, seeking out faces, imagining himself happily fitting in, a single spoke in the large wheel of a real family.

His favorite picture was of an Italian family. There was a boy with a cap on his head and a sack over his shoulder. Beside the boy stood a little girl and a mother with a baby in her arms. Dominic thought the boy looked like him with his dark hair and eyes. He spent a long time in front of the picture, not only imagining himself a part of this family, but imagining that this boy was somehow *really* his Italian ancestor. He realized this was a one-in-a-million chance. But he couldn't stop thinking, *what if?*

After Dominic had stared at the picture for a long time, he decided to go upstairs to the third floor and see what there might be to do up there. But as he started to climb the now motionless escalator, a low, mechanical groan suddenly arose from the silent steps, and he jumped off.

Then, just as suddenly as it had started up, the noise stopped. Everything was quiet again, a deadly quiet that chilled Dominic to the bone.

Dazed with fear, he stumbled about the room and bumped into a display case, which caused him to scream out loud. The unexpected noise had shaken his nerves so badly that his teeth had begun to chatter.

What was going on? he wondered. *Was someone there? Were they watching him and trying to frighten him?*

Crouching under a display stand of telephones, Dominic squeezed his eyes shut tight and willed his teeth to stop chattering. He sat perfectly still, like a hunted animal, hiding, waiting, and listening. But the low hum of the air conditioning was the only sound to fill the room. Dominic stayed that way for what seemed like hours, frozen with fear, until he felt his legs begin to cramp.

Slowly, cautiously, he moved out from under the table and finally stood up. Then without thinking, he reached out and picked up one of the telephone receivers on the display in front of him. An old Norwegian man talked about his homeland. Dominic was filled with such relief that he let out a loud sigh. It was the first human voice he had heard all night. And even though he knew that it was only a tape, the sound of the old man was somehow comforting.

. As he went from one telephone to another, Dominic's fear slipped away, and he began to pretend that he was actually having conversations with the voices. They were mostly old people, grandmothers and grandfathers he guessed. He pretended they were his. Soon he began to feel less lonely.

But the voices never answered him, and after a while he began to long to talk to someone real, someone who would answer his questions and listen to what he had to say, like a real grandmother or grandfather would have.

Dominic's hand reached for the last phone on the stand, when the flashlight went dead. Suddenly he was in total darkness. Frantically, he tapped the flashlight against the table, and turned the switch on and off, but it was no use. It wouldn't light up. He dropped it down onto the display stand.

Desperately frightened, Dominic stood trembling in the blackness. His hand searched under his T-shirt until his fingers felt the familiar smooth curves of his lucky key. What was he supposed to do now? Where could he go? What if someone was out there, watching him, waiting for him?

Dominic reached back down for the useless flashlight, thinking to carry it as a weapon if he had to, but his hand fell over the phone receiver instead. It was the last phone on the stand, the one he was about to pick up before the flashlight died. He brought the receiver to his ear and heard a kindly old voice begin to speak.

"I came to America when I was a boy of eleven years old."

"I'm all alone," Dominic blurted out. "And nobody cares. Nobody even came to look for me."

"In Italy we had very little, and yet we had so much."

"I don't know what to do." Dominic's voice was choked with sobs. "The flashlight is broken and it's so dark. I'm afraid, I'm afraid . . ."

"My brothers and I all shared one pair of shoes. We had to take turns wearing them."

"Mr. Howard forgot me and maybe my foster family forgot me, too."

"In Italy we had a goat."

"Oh, please. It's so dark and I'm so afraid," Dominic pleaded. "Please, listen to me." There was a long pause on the other end.

Then, as he stood all alone in the darkness, Dominic Cantori heard the old voice whisper, "Yes, little one, I'm listening."

CHAPTER SIX

DOMINIC HELD HIS BREATH as his trembling fingers tightened around the phone. Had he really heard what he thought he'd heard? He pressed the receiver to his ear and waited.

"W-were you talking to me?" he finally managed to stammer.

"Yes, little one," the old voice replied. "I'm talking to you."

Dominic felt his heart pound in his chest. How could a tape recording answer his questions? Who was talking to him? And what did he want?

As Dominic tried to unravel this mystery, the escalator suddenly gave out another loud groan. The sound of clashing metal echoed off the walls of the empty hall.

"I'm so scared," Dominic whimpered. "I've never been so scared. I don't know what's happening."

"Try to be brave. I'm here with you now, and I

won't leave you," the voice on the other end promised.

The old man's words enveloped him like an embrace. The voice was so calm and gentle that it gave him the courage to speak.

"Who are you?"

"I came into this world with my father's name, Francesco Candiano," the voice answered. "I know how you are feeling, because, like you, I found myself lost and afraid in this very same building. Of course, that was many years ago, when I was just a boy. I had made the journey from Italy. Our family was so very poor."

"I never knew my family," Dominic whispered. "And I really don't know where they're from. My caseworker, Dave, says that I have to keep hoping that he'll find a permanent family, but I don't know if I can. I don't know if he'll ever find a family that wants me."

"Ah," the old man sighed.

"I'm so afraid my class will find out," Dominic explained, fighting back the tears. "I couldn't stand for everyone to know, so that's why I lied. But then it all backfired when the ranger started talking about the wall and I had to hide. I don't know what to do now. I'm trapped in here and I don't know what to do."

"You're doing fine." Francesco Candiano's voice was soft and smooth as velvet. Dominic relaxed his grip on the receiver. He closed his eyes and took a deep breath as the old man continued.

"Many, many people have walked through these halls feeling frightened and alone. Coming to a new country is like being adopted into a new family. As I made my way through this building I can remember thinking much like you. But somehow I found the courage to keep going. You have more courage than you know, my young friend."

"But I don't feel brave," Dominic whispered. "How can I have courage if I'm feeling so scared?"

"Your courage is there, right alongside of your fear. That makes it hard, I know. I myself was terrified when I had to leave our village."

"Where was that?" Dominic asked.

"Across the ocean, in Italy," Mr. Candiano told him. "Imagine, if you can, a little village perched high on a cliff just above a spread of lemon groves. That was Avaletto. And below those gardens the shimmering blue of the sea. Such a sight! Those lemon-scented hills, spilling over with wild roses and grapes, were my home. I can still hear the canaries singing in the mornings along with the bells from the cathedral of Sant' Andrea. All the beauty you could want for a lifetime was in that little village."

"But if it was so beautiful, why did you leave?"

"Ah, beauty," the old man replied. "As much as it is able to feed the soul, it can't feed an empty belly. It was a hard life, you see. The year was 1908. We didn't have what you had in this country then. We were very poor. As beautiful as those songbirds sounded, the best sound of all was the quiet of a satisfied stomach. So we ate them."

"You ate the canaries?"

"There was so little food."

Dominic rubbed his eyes. He was suddenly feeling sleepy again.

"So little, and yet so very much," the old man continued. "There was much I had to leave behind. The sound of Father Tomaso's laugh, the warm, sweet smile of my Violetta, and the scent of lemons on those sun-kissed hillsides. So much to leave behind . . ."

"Why don't you go back to see them?" Dominic asked.

"Oh, I do," Mr. Candiano said. "In my dreams. I return to them all in my dreams."

"Your dreams?" asked Dominic sleepily.

"For Father Tomaso has been dead a long time now. And my dear Violetta as well. Yes, they're all gone."

"My family is gone, too," Dominic said.

"You've had a rough time. You need to rest now, little one. Go ahead and rest," the old man gently commanded.

As he leaned his head against the display case, Dominic was overcome by a drowsiness he'd never experienced before. He struggled to stay awake. He wanted to ask what was happening, but sleep was now too powerful to resist. Dominic could no longer keep his eyes open. All he could do was listen as the gentle, old voice whispered, soft as a lullaby, in his ear:

"Open your heart and all that you need shall be yours. Listen now, you can hear the bells of Sant' Andrea. . . ."

CHAPTER
SEVEN

DOMINIC STRUGGLED to raise his head, but he couldn't move. In the darkness he felt a deep rumbling in the floor beneath him. He knew he wasn't moving, and yet he had the strangest sensation of speeding through space. It went on and on, and each time Dominic tried to stand, he went crashing to the floor. After what seemed like a very long time, the sensation stopped and a cool breeze washed over his face. From a distance came the sound of bells. Dominic took a deep breath and lifted his head.

"Lemons," he whispered. "I smell lemons." Dominic's eyes slowly opened. He reached out with his hands and felt warm, damp blades of grass and the soft petals of wildflowers beneath his fingers.

He took another whiff of the air. The refreshing scent tickled his nose. He had never smelled air this fresh and clean. He blinked his eyes, and in the early morning light he was startled to realize that he was sitting high on a cliff! How did he get here? Where was he? As questions raced through his mind, Dominic scrambled to his feet and made his way to the meadow's edge to see the dazzling view before him.

The terraced hillsides below were woven with a tapestry of tiled red roofs and whitewashed houses that clung to the cliffs. Buttery, yellow wildflowers and scarlet poppies spilled over fence rows. All this was edged in crumbling stone walls that wove their way down to the sparkling blue of the sea.

As Dominic stared, the old man's words suddenly came back to him: "All the beauty you could want for a lifetime was in that little village."

CHAPTER EIGHT

"Where am I?" Dominic cried aloud. "Where am I?"

"If you get any closer to the edge of that cliff, you'll be in the sea," came a voice behind him.

Dominic immediately recognized that the words he was hearing were in Italian. One of the foster homes he lived in was in an Italian section of Brooklyn. The people in his favorite bakery spoke Italian all the time, but he had never been able to understand them. And yet somehow, now, he understood every word that had been spoken.

He spun around to find a thin boy about his own age standing a few feet away. The boy was wearing brown woolen shorts and no shirt. His skin was deeply tanned, and his shoeless feet were dirty and stained. Two small dead canaries dangled from a string that was tied to the belt loop of his shorts.

Beside him stood two younger boys. The youngest, a boy of about seven years old, had a head of blond curls and what appeared to be a small, brightly painted accordion slung over his shoulder. The other boy looked a few years older. He had dark hair and dark eyes. Over his shoulder was a coil of thick rope netting. Both of the younger boys were dressed much the same, in raggedy shorts and dirty shirts.

As they came nearer, there was a strong scent of sweat mixed with smoke. Their grimy arms and legs were covered in scratches, and their hair was matted and unbrushed.

"Are you hunting in our territory?" the oldest boy demanded.

"Me?" Dominic sputtered. "Hunting? No!" He was equally shocked to hear his own words coming out in Italian. The three boys circled about him.

"His clothes are strange," the youngest boy said, pointing to his T-shirt. "Did you paint that sea monster on your shirt?"

"What?" Dominic asked, looking down at the Tyrannosaurus Rex on the front of his shirt. "No, it's not a sea monster, it's a dinosaur."

The boys grew quiet as they stared.

"What is a dinosaur?" the oldest boy asked.

"I never met a kid who didn't know what a dinosaur was," Dominic answered. "Dinosaurs are animals that lived long ago in prehistoric times," he told them. "This one on my shirt is T. Rex. He was one of the mightiest dinosaurs ever. Haven't you heard of T. Rex?"

The boys shook their heads.

"Look how clean his hands are," the boy with the net on his shoulder said, picking up one of Dominic's hands and examining it. "He must be the son of a *padrone,* one of the bosses."

"What is your name and what village is your family from?" the older boy demanded.

"My family?"

Dominic was too dazed to make another story up. "They're all dead," he said. "My name is Dominic. I have no family and I don't know where I am."

On hearing this, the boys softened and looked at him with great sympathy.

"Our village, Avaletto, is down there," the youngest boy said, pointing down the hillside, through a grove of olive trees.

"Avaletto?" Dominic tried to remember where he had heard that name before. "There is no countryside like this in Brooklyn. We must be in an Italian neighborhood in New Jersey."

"New Jersey?" the older boy repeated slowly. He shook his head. "I have never heard of that village, but then I don't know all the villages in Italy," he said.

"Italy?" Dominic whispered.

"Where else would we be?" the youngest boy replied with a smile, as two dimples appeared on his cheeks.

Dominic was too stunned to answer. As he went over in his mind all that had happened that day, a chill raced down his spine. "Do you know an old man who lives in your village?" he asked.

"Avaletto is full of old men," the middle boy answered. "They're the only men who are left here. They say that in some villages, so many people have gone, there is no one left to light the lamps. They have all gone to America."

"America?"

"Yes, they say the streets in America are paved with gold," the oldest boy told him. Then he turned to look over his shoulder. "Violetta," he called. "Violetta, where have you gone?"

"Violetta?" Dominic whispered.

"A beautiful name, hey?" The boy's suntanned face broke into a wide grin. "Wait until you meet her. She's a beauty."

"What is your name?" Dominic asked.

"Forgive us for not introducing ourselves sooner," the boy said. "These are my brothers. Antonio is seven," he said, pointing to the youngest boy with the blond curls and dimples. "And this is Salvatore."

"I'm ten years old," Salvatore announced as he adjusted the net on his shoulder.

Dominic felt another shiver race down his spine as he heard the boy say, "And I'm Francesco. Francesco Candiano."

CHAPTER
NINE

DOMINIC FIXED HIS EYES on the oldest boy. Wasn't Francesco Candiano the name of the old man he'd just heard on the display phone in the museum? But how could that be?

"What year is it?" Dominic asked, hoping his question wouldn't sound too strange.

Francesco shook his head. "May the saints protect us," he said, rolling his big dark eyes to the sky, and making the sign of the cross. "What was it?" he asked gently. "An accident of some kind?"

"Or maybe," Salvatore whispered, "*il malocchio,* the evil eye, has been placed on him!"

"I don't know what happened," Dominic tried to explain. "I was talking to an old man. It was so dark, and then I heard a rumbling noise and the ground began to shake. I don't remember anything after that."

"Ah, so that's it," Francesco said. "The dark, the rumbling noise, the floor shaking. Don't you see? It must have been the earthquake down in Calabria." He turned to look at Dominic. "Is that why you're dressed so strangely? Have the Gypsies dressed you?"

Dominic was about to answer, when Salvatore interrupted.

"But the earthquake was a long time ago. Have you been wandering around like this since then?"

"What year was it?" Dominic asked.

"This year, of course," Francesco answered.

"Yes, I know, but what year is this year?" Dominic's voice cracked with anxiety. "Just tell me what year it is," he begged.

"It's 1908," Antonio squeaked. "Anyone knows that."

CHAPTER TEN

"OH, NO!" DOMINIC CRIED. "He's taken me back! The old man has taken me back into his dream!"

"I still say it sounds like *il malocchio* to me," Salvatore said, shaking his head.

Antonio and Salvatore began to pick up stones from the ground.

"Make sure there are thirteen of them," Francesco ordered. He turned to Dominic and whispered. "Don't worry, we'll fill your pockets."

"What are you talking about?" Dominic asked.

"If the evil eye has been placed on you," Francesco explained, "you need to wear a horn, or carry thirteen stones. Thirteen is a lucky number. It wards off evil. We have no horn, so you'll have to use the thirteen stones. But I don't believe it was *il malocchio*. I think it was the earthquake."

Confused by all the talk of evil eyes and earthquakes and the thought that he had somehow gone back in time, Dominic reached for his lucky key and let out a horrified cry when he discovered it was gone.

"Calm down," Francesco said. "You're very mixed up right now."

"No, you don't understand," Dominic protested. "I've lost it! The only thing I've ever cared about."

"Yes, you've lost your family, I know," Francesco said gently. "We three are orphans like you. We, too, have lost our parents."

For a moment, Dominic forgot about his lost key and stared at Francesco and his brothers. He'd never met other orphans. He'd always been the only one in his class, whichever class he was in.

As he stared, he noticed how these boys looked so dirty and unkempt. They looked much worse off than he had ever been.

"No, no, that's not what I meant," he answered. "Listen to me. I'm not from here. This is all a dream. It's the old man's dream."

"If it is a dream, why don't you just wake up?"

Dominic thought this over and decided it was worth a try. Closing his eyes as tight as he could, he took a deep breath. "All I have to do is will myself to wake up. I'm going to wake up now, and this is all going to be gone and I'll be back at the museum," he whispered.

Sitting perfectly still, Dominic concentrated as

hard as he could. He counted to ten and opened one eye.

Francesco shook his head. "Some dreamer," he said. "Is this the best you can do? If this were my dream, I'd have a pirate ship, silver swords, and a bowl of mussel soup. And some pasta with garlic sauce, and some sweet *panettone,* sweet cake, for dessert."

"Oh, no," Dominic moaned, opening his other eye. "You're not real. I know you're not real."

"What the old men in the village say is true." Francesco shrugged. "You live at the toe of the boot and you go crazy from the stink."

"Boot? Toe? What are you talking about?"

"Haven't you learned your geography yet? Even in a little hill town like Avaletto, we know of such things. This land is shaped like a boot, and Calabria, where you come from, is in the toe of the boot."

"But I never said I came from there," Dominic protested. "I told you I . . ."

"Sure, sure, I know, you're from a dream," Francesco said with a wave of his hand. "Listen, *mio amico*. Listen, my friend. The earthquake has given you a bad shock." Francesco gently placed his arm around Dominic's shoulder. "That is enough to rattle anyone's head." He knocked on Dominic's forehead with his knuckles.

Dominic leaned away from Francesco. He was

not used to anyone touching him or being so familiar.

"Look out!" Antonio suddenly shouted.

Dominic had no sooner turned his head to look when he heard the jangle of a bell and his face met with a blur of white fur. Francesco reached out to grab him as he was about to fall off the wall he had been sitting on. Dominic sat back up and found himself staring into the amused, dark eyes of a goat.

"Violetta! I am surprised at you," Francesco scolded. "Is that any way to greet a stranger?"

Dominic sat up with a start as the goat lowered her head demurely and began to lick his hand with her long, pebbly pink tongue. With a graceful upward motion she raised her head back up and burped in his ear.

With a shock, Dominic thought about how it had only been yesterday that he had been back at the museum, wishing for someone to burp in his ear! Now it all seemed like light years away. There was so much that he didn't understand. How did he get here? How was he to get back? Why were these boys filling his pockets with stones? And who was this goat that was burping in his ear?

CHAPTER
ELEVEN

WITH ANOTHER GRACEFUL TILT of her head, Violetta nibbled on the shoulder of Dominic's T-shirt and let out a bleat and a burp.

"She burped again!" Dominic exclaimed.

"It's one of her many talents," Francesco bragged. "It's her song of contentment."

"Oh, Francesco, why must you always play the poet?" Salvatore groaned. "Why can't you just say your goat burps?"

"Anyone can see that she's a very contented goat," Francesco replied.

"I'd be content, too, if I could eat anything in sight," Salvatore said.

Francesco buried his face in Violetta's neck. "She's as gentle as a lamb. And quite musical, too, hey?"

Dominic nodded and reached out to pet Violetta's neck. Between her bleating and her burping she really did sound musical. He thought about all the pets he had dreamed of having, but he'd never dreamed of a pet goat!

"I pray to Saint Francis every day to keep her healthy," Francesco continued.

"Saint Francis?" Dominic asked.

"Yes." Francesco nodded. "Father Tomaso says that Saint Francis of Assisi loved animals so much that when he talked to them, they answered. Because of this miracle, he is the patron saint of animals everywhere, isn't that right, Violetta?"

Violetta tilted her head, yawned a big yawn, and then began to nibble again on Dominic's T-shirt.

"Even if a miracle was visited on her, Violetta wouldn't talk," Salvatore joked. "She'd be too busy eating."

Violetta's tug at the hem of his shirt tickled Dominic.

"One day, Saint Francis may decide to bless Violetta with a miracle," Francesco declared. "And then won't you be sorry, Salvatore, for mocking her so."

"Hey, she really is hungry!" Dominic cried. The boys all laughed as Dominic tugged his shirt away from Violetta's teeth.

"She does try to eat anything in sight," Francesco admitted, sitting down on a moss-covered rock. "But I think she likes you."

"I like you, too," Dominic whispered as Violetta nuzzled against his leg.

"There is no better pet in the world," Francesco remarked.

"I always wanted a sheep dog," Dominic said, thinking of his dream family.

"A dog?" Francesco scoffed. "How can you say such a thing? A dog could never be as smart as Violetta."

"And you couldn't get a drink from a dog," Antonio pointed out.

"A drink?" Dominic watched Antonio squeeze underneath Violetta's belly.

"Antonio, where are your manners?" Francesco scolded, grabbing hold of his little brother's shirt. "Guests go first."

Dominic's eyes grew wide as he realized that Francesco was talking about drinking from the goat!

"No, no, that's all right," Dominic assured them. "I can wait, really."

I can wait for a can of soda from a soda machine, or a glass of normal cow's milk from the refrigerator, he thought. Then he realized that if this really was the year 1908, such things as modern refrigerators and soda machines hadn't even been invented yet.

Francesco let go of Antonio's shirt. As the bright sun beat down on his head, Dominic gulped. Now that he thought about it, he found that his mouth was dry and his throat was parched. He watched as Francesco began to squeeze one of Violetta's long pinkish teats. Soon a thin stream of milk came squirting out, and Antonio was quick to catch it in his mouth.

Dominic licked his lips and wondered just what goat milk tasted like. Salvatore threw off the heavy netting from his shoulder and crouched down beside Violetta for his turn.

"Why do you carry that with you?" Dominic asked, trying to get his mind off his thirst.

"We worked for the *padrone* picking lemons last week, and he paid us in trade," Salvatore explained, wiping the milk from his mouth.

"The *padrone?*"

"Padrone Pirozzi owns what's left of the lemon trees there," Francesco said, pointing to the orchard below them. In the bright morning light Dominic could see the lemon trees clinging to the hillside. He took a deep breath and the faint fragrance of lemons tickled his nose.

"Since the blight killed off many of the trees, the workers have all gone and the *padrone* has no one to pick the fruit that's left," Salvatore continued.

"We picked him forty bushels yesterday and all we got was this old net full of holes," Francesco grumbled.

"I think I can mend it, if I can get a big enough

needle," Salvatore declared, spreading the net on the ground. Violetta was quick to begin nibbling on its worn edges.

"Will you stop!" Salvatore shouted angrily, pulling her away.

"Salvatore, why must you always lose that temper of yours?" Francesco sighed.

"Oh, and what would you have me do?" Salvatore retorted. "I should smile as she chews up a day's work?"

"Violetta is an intelligent animal," Francesco reminded him. "You don't need to shout for her to understand you."

Violetta lost interest in the net and began to turn her attention to the fringe on Salvatore's shorts.

"I wish I could eat anything, like Violetta," Antonio complained. "My stomach is so empty that it hurts all the time."

Dominic suddenly thought of his own stomach and of how hungry he had become.

"Don't complain, Antonio," scolded Francesco. "You just had a drink of milk. Be thankful for that."

"But I'm still hungry," Antonio moaned. "Can we roast the birds, now?"

"No, we'll wait until we can get two more. They're so small there's hardly a mouthful here for one of us," Francesco decided.

Dominic thought about the foster families he stayed with and how he didn't always like the meals they made. He thought about all the times he had gone to bed hungry, rather than try some of their strange-looking chili or tuna casserole. Now he would gladly have eaten any of those.

"What about the family you stay with?" Dominic asked. "Don't you like the food they give you?"

"We don't have a family to stay with," Francesco explained. "We sleep in a hayloft in one of the *padrone's* barns. It's a good, dry place to sleep. Father Tomaso gives us bread once a week and once a month we get some pork or beef. The rest of the time we must find food wherever we can.

"Father Tomaso looks after the orphans in these hills," Salvatore added. "And he has even found some of them families in America."

Dominic felt his heart leap at the mention of America.

"Father Tomaso has promised to find us such a family one day," Antonio piped in. "Have you ever had a family to stay with?"

Dominic squirmed. He wasn't used to talking about himself. "Sure," he replied. "I've had lots of families." The other boys grew quiet on hearing this. From the looks on the brothers' faces, Dominic could tell that they were impressed, and he didn't want this moment of being envied to end.

"Did these families feed you?" Antonio asked. Dominic nodded.

"Where are they now?" Salvatore demanded. "Are they looking for other children? Are they down south in Calabria?"

Dominic struggled to fight back his tears. It was all so confusing. He wanted so much to tell them the truth, but how could they understand?

"I'm not from Calabria," he began. "My home, where I come from it's . . . it's far away," he stammered. "It's across the ocean. It's across time, too. I know you won't believe me, but I was born in America. It's where I live, it's where I got my shirt. I live in the future — about a hundred years from now."

The three Candiano brothers stared at him wide-eyed. Antonio's mouth had dropped open and the only thing to break their stunned silence were the sounds of Violetta chewing and bleating, and singing her song of contentment.

CHAPTER TWELVE

FRANCESCO SIGHED. "You are more confused than I thought."

"It's like I told you . . . about this old man and his dream . . ." Dominic tried to explain.

"Oh, no," Francesco interrupted. "We're back to that dream, hey? Well, all right, if you are as you say in a dream, why not relax? Soon you'll wake up, and everything will be as it always was. So there's really nothing to worry about, is there?"

"Well . . ." Dominic hesitated. "I guess . . ."

Suddenly Dominic's worries were interrupted.

"*Ciao*, Francesco! Hello!" A young girl's voice called from the distance. Dominic and the others turned to see a dark-haired girl in a dirty, raggedy dress running toward them, followed by a small flock of sheep.

"*Ciao*, Nina!" Francesco called his greeting back to her.

"I've been looking all over for you!" the girl

exclaimed as she ran up to them. Her face was flushed and bits of raw wool stuck to her long, dark braids.

"What's the matter, Nina? Did you miss Francesco?" Salvatore teased. Francesco blushed at this remark.

"It's not me who wants to see you," the girl scoffed. "It's Father Tomaso. He has been looking everywhere for you. He says that you're to come at once." She turned to look at Dominic. "Who is your friend?" she asked with a smile. "And why is he dressed so strangely?"

"*Il malocchio* is on him," Salvatore whispered dramatically. "And that demon he wears on his shirt will put the evil eye on you if you look at it."

On hearing this Nina's smile faded and she took a step backward.

"Don't listen to Salvatore," Francesco told her. He went on to explain about the earthquake and how confused Dominic was. Nina listened, then she reached into the cloth pouch that hung from her waist and pulled something out. She offered it to Dominic.

"*Mangia! Mangia!*" Nina coaxed. "Eat! Eat!" She unwrapped the grape leaves that covered a large piece of cheese. "From my sheep," Nina told him as she nodded to the ewe standing beside her.

Dominic took a bite of the cheese. It was the

first food he had eaten since the day before, and even though the cheese was sharper and more pungent than the American cheese he was used to eating, Dominic was glad to have something to put into his empty stomach.

Antonio was quick to ask for a piece, and Salvatore followed.

"How is your baby doing?" Francesco asked as a little black and white lamb nuzzled against Nina's leg.

Nina's face broke into a smile. She knelt down beside the lamb and he licked her cheek.

"My little Galileo. Do you see how strong his legs are? He can outrun some of the older ewes already!"

Dominic could see how proud Nina was of her lamb. He reached out to pet Galileo's soft woolly back, and was suddenly reminded of how much he wanted a pet of his own to be proud of and to take care of.

"I have to get my sheep to the pasture," Nina said as she stood up. "And don't forget to stop in to see Father Tomaso? He said it was urgent."

Francesco shook his head. "We're on our way there now," he promised, waving good-bye to her.

"*Buon giorno,* Nina, good day," the boys called after her.

"We will take you with us to see Father Tomaso," Francesco told Dominic. "He is the most beloved priest around here. If there is a way to help you, Father Tomaso will find it." He put his arm around Dominic. "You can come along with us, what do you say?"

"Okay," Dominic mumbled, pulling away from Francesco. He didn't know if he'd ever get used to all the touching, but he was glad for their company.

As he followed behind them, Dominic couldn't take his eyes off of the countryside. Having grown up in the city, Dominic was used to city streets, the noise of traffic, doors slamming, people shouting, and the bus fumes lingering about street corners. Here he found himself surrounded by the gentle curves of the green hills, the sound of birds overhead, and the earthy scents of lemons and herbs in the air.

"Shh, listen," said Salvatore, coming to a sudden stop.

Dominic stopped and listened along with the others. He could just make out the faint tinkling of bells in the distance.

"Donkey bells," Salvatore whispered. "That's most likely Dominica, Randizzi's donkey. We saw them yesterday carrying stones up for the *padrone's* new wine house. The orchard is empty."

"Who is Randizzi?" Dominic asked.

"He is the giant who works for the *padrone*. He is in charge of this hillside," Francesco told him.

"He is bigger than three men," Salvatore added. "With a heart no bigger than a thumbnail. Anyone caught stealing fruit or hunting on the land must answer to his whip."

"Whip?" Dominic gulped.

"He dips it in lye," Antonio whispered. "So as to leave his mark for good. Show him the scar, Salvatore."

Salvatore turned around and pulled up his shirt. Dominic winced at the sight of the long, thin scar that striped Salvatore's back.

"Don't worry," Francesco said, on seeing Dominic's anxious face. "We won't be meeting Randizzi's whip today. Look for yourself. It's as Salvatore said, the orchard is empty."

Dominic followed his gaze to see a small orchard at the end of the path. Three large trees were covered in deep ruby-red cherries, and the air held the heady scent of their fruit.

"Come on," Francesco called as he and Violetta took off at a trot.

Salvatore quickly threw off the heavy net from his shoulder and began to climb one of the trees.

Dominic had never stolen anything before, and the idea of stealing from a giant with a whip made his stomach more than a little queasy. But it was his almost-empty stomach that gave him the courage he needed now. He had not eaten anything since breakfast the day before in New York, and the little bit of cheese that Nina had given him hadn't made a dent in his mounting hunger.

He watched as Francesco took the birds off his belt and slung them over a low branch of a tree.

Dominic knew that, as hungry as he was, he wouldn't be able to eat those little birds. He decided instead to eat as many cherries as he could. He watched Antonio shinny up the tree behind Salvatore. Together the two boys threw the cherries down. And soon they all sat under the tree, filling their empty bellies with the delicious sweet fruit.

"Francesco, can we roast the birds now? I'm still hungry," Antonio whined.

"Shame on you, Antonio," Francesco scolded. "You are never satisfied. No, we'll save the birds for our evening meal."

"Don't worry, Antonio," Salvatore told him. "I heard yesterday that Signor Falcone, the baker, has a rat problem in his shop again. He'll trade bread and *biscotti* for every rat we catch. I'm going to try to catch some rats. Maybe I'll be lucky."

Dominic remembered the long hard cookies called "biscotti" from the Italian bakery in one of his old neighborhoods.

He wanted to hear more about the rats and the

biscotti, but Antonio had spit a cherry pit so far that it hit a tree a good distance away.

"I'll bet you can't top that," Antonio bragged.

Francesco and Dominic were quick to try, and soon they had a pit spitting contest, with everyone taking part but Salvatore.

"Salvatore, how many times must I tell you not to swallow the pits?" Francesco scolded.

"What's wrong with pits?" his brother retorted. "At least they fill me up."

"You're going to end up with one taking root in your stomach," Francesco told him.

"Salvatore is going to have a tree growing out of his nose." Antonio giggled as he pulled an imaginary tree from Salvatore's nose.

Salvatore gave him a gentle shove and Antonio shoved back and soon all the boys were wrestling on the ground like frisky puppies. Antonio stopped suddenly when he saw a stub of bread fall out of Salvatore's pocket.

"Where did you get that?" Antonio asked.

Salvatore shrugged, "I found it by the well."

"And you told no one about it?" Francesco's voice was stern.

"I forgot," Salvatore said weakly.

"Give it to me," Francesco ordered. His brother was quick to hand over the bread.

"How many times must I tell you?" Francesco sighed, pulling the bread apart. "We are a *famiglia*.

We are family. And as a family we share all we have. We may not have much, but if we forget each other, then we have nothing. Do you understand?"

Salvatore's eyes welled with tears, ashamed at having his own greed exposed before the little group. Francesco passed out the pieces of bread, which the boys quickly devoured. Dominic was glad that Francesco had included him. It was only a mouthful, but it satisfied more than his hunger. It felt wonderful to be included in their family.

As Dominic popped another cherry into his mouth, his thoughts drifted back to his own time. He thought about how poor he often felt with his shabby clothes and old sneakers. But he realized that he had never been as poor as these boys.

He was never so hungry that he had to kill birds for his supper. He never had to steal in order to eat. He never had to trap a rat to get a cookie. And he never had to fill his stomach with cherry pits, because there was nothing else to fill it. Dominic suddenly realized just how desperate these boys were for food. But at the same time, being with the three raggedly dressed brothers, who considered him family, made him feel richer than he had ever felt before.

When they finished eating the cherries, Francesco called for a song.

"Antonio" he ordered. "Play us something on your concertina."

Antonio picked up the little wooden instrument and soon the air was filled with a cheerful melody. Listening to Antonio's gentle tune against the sound of the wind in the trees, Dominic thought of how different the sounds were back at home. The music he liked listening to had only come out of his Walkman, or a television, or a stereo.

And the sounds outdoors were of cars and buses speeding by, boomboxes blasting on the sidewalks, grinding screeches of the subway, and noisy jet planes crisscrossing through the skies overhead.

But here in this place and time, in the Italy of 1908, there were no such sounds. Here Dominic listened along with the others to the tinkle of donkey bells in the distance, the sweet notes from Antonio's concertina, and the rustling of the olive leaves in the wind.

There was a calmness to this place, a gentleness that seemed so different from the modern city life he had always known.

"Hey, Tullio!" a voice suddenly shouted. "Do you smell the armpit of an orphan Gypsy?"

CHAPTER THIRTEEN

"*SAN GENNARO, PENSACI TU!* Saint Gennaro, protect us!" Francesco whispered as he crossed himself. Then he and the others turned to see four boys swaggering toward them down the path. One of the boys carried a piglet.

"Who are they?" Dominic whispered as the boys drew closer.

"The one with the piglet in his arms is Sausage Pirozzi," Francesco said, hurrying to his feet. "He is the son of the *padrone*. Because he can afford to eat so much sausage, he does, and so he has ended up looking like one."

"He always carries that piglet around to show how rich he is," Salvatore added as he collected his net. "He and his cousin, Tullio, the one he's with, think they are better than the rest of us because they eat meat every week."

"Ugh! What's that smell?" Sausage called out.

"I smell moldy barnyard straw," Tullio retorted.

Salvatore took a step forward, his face crimson with anger. But Francesco was quick to pull him back.

"Ignore them," Francesco whispered in his ear. "Remember what Father Tomaso told us. Turn your other cheek. You know how Father says that it takes more strength not to fight than to fight."

"Stealing fruit again from my papa's orchard?" Sausage asked, clicking his tongue while giving his piglet a squeeze. "I think maybe I should send for Signor Randizzi. Do you suppose that's what I should do?"

"It was only a few cherries," Francesco said, trying to reason with him. "We won't take any more."

"Once a thief, always a thief. It is how you are made," Sausage retorted.

"Hey, Sausage, *tu sei un fungo!* You are made like a mushroom," Salvatore replied.

"Nello!" Sausage shouted to a younger boy beside him. "Go and fetch Signor Randizzi. Tell him we have visitors in our orchard."

"Too bad we'll have to miss him," Francesco said with a nervous smile. "We were just leaving." He whistled for Violetta and took Antonio by the hand. "Salvatore, grab the birds," he whispered.

Salvatore picked up the canaries and Dominic followed behind them as they began walking forward toward the path. But Sausage and his group had spread out, blocking their way.

"Hold your noses, everyone," Sausage taunted. "There's a bad stink in the air. And look, they've found another bad smell to join them."

Dominic stood frozen, expressionless, the way he always did when kids taunted him.

"I'd rather smell old Giuseppina's donkey stall," Sausage said, holding his nose.

Tullio and the others laughed at this.

"It is you who smells, Sausage," Salvatore shouted back. "With all that fish oil you rub on those old shoes of yours, everyone can smell you before you come into sight."

"At least I own a pair of shoes all to myself," Sausage retorted.

"Maybe you should try some fish oil yourselves," shouted Tullio. "It might help to cover up the stink. Or maybe this will do."

With that he reached down to the ground, picked up a dried clump of manure, and threw it their way. Two other boys in their group followed Tullio's lead and armed themselves with stones for ammunition.

"Ignore them," Francesco ordered as they took shelter behind a tree. But on hearing another slur, Salvatore spun around and threw a clod of manure, just missing Tullio's arm. As a large stone flew through the air, Salvatore tried to return the fire, only to miss his mark once more.

"Salvatore," Francesco shouted. "How many times must I tell you?"

"I know, I know," Salvatore yelled, throwing another clod. "Aim for the other cheek."

"Turn the other cheek!" Francesco cried, pulling Antonio behind a bush. "Not aim for it!"

Dominic ducked down low with the others as another clod of manure flew over their heads. Suddenly the sound of donkey bells could be heard coming up the path.

"Oh, no! It's Dominica!" Antonio gasped.

"We must leave now!" Francesco exclaimed.

"But they've blocked the path!" Salvatore cried.

"Then we'll just have to make a run for it through the orchard," Francesco shouted.

"Quick! They're getting away!" Sausage yelled as Salvatore and Francesco ran in the other direction. Dominic and Antonio followed behind them. With Violetta at their side and a barrage of stones at their backs, the boys raced through the orchard, running as fast as their feet would take them.

"Run! Run!" Francesco cried.

And run they did. They ran straight into the trap set for them, straight into the path of the giant, Randizzi!

"Stop there!" a thunderous voice bellowed as Dominic felt his knees begin to buckle.

CHAPTER FOURTEEN

FRANCESCO AND SALVATORE had managed to escape into the bushes, but Dominic and Antonio weren't so lucky. Together they stood frozen with fear before the biggest, scariest-looking man that Dominic had ever seen.

Tibero Randizzi was a mountainous creature with a broad, hairy chest that burst the seams of his black leather vest. His long, tree trunk-like legs carried his torso high into the air. His voice was a thunderous roar. In his powerful fist, Randizzi gripped the polished wooden handle of a homemade whip. Its long, thin branches had been sharpened into razorlike points, and dusted with lye.

Suddenly, with his free hand, Randizzi grabbed Antonio by the scruff of his neck. "Now I have you," he growled, his thick lips curling into a snarl. "And I'll whip you for all the fruit you've stolen today, yesterday, and the day before that."

Antonio's face had gone white, and his eyes were glassy with fear.

"Let him go," Dominic shouted, taking a step closer to them. His heart raced, and his breath quickened. Dominic had never been so frightened in his life, but he couldn't stop moving closer!

"Let him go!" he shouted again. "I stole the cherries."

"Oh, so you want to take his place?" Randizzi laughed as he let go of Antonio and grabbed hold of Dominic's neck. Sausage and the others cheered.

"You have a little more meat on your bones, anyway," hissed Randizzi as Dominic struggled to get his breath. Seconds later the giant had released his vise-like grip on Dominic's neck, and was throwing him over his lap.

"More skin for my lashes to mark," he growled.

Dominic felt faint as he caught sight of the long whip being raised into the air. He closed his eyes tight on hearing the loud *whoosh* as it came down and ripped through his thin T-shirt, opening the skin on his back. A deadly silence followed as Sausage and the others were stilled by the frightening sight of Randizzi's handiwork.

Then, with a satisfied grunt, the giant lifted his whip once more. Just at that moment, a flying clod of manure sailed through the air and struck him on the back of his bald head.

Seething with anger, Tibero Randizzi stood up, letting Dominic fall to the ground. The giant took one step forward, but then tripped and let out a pained cry. Everyone looked on in astonishment as he lay slumped on the ground moaning and clutching his chest.

While Sausage and his group ran to Randizzi's side, Dominic grabbed Antonio's hand and the two took off.

"Stop! Thieves! Stinking thieves!" Sausage shouted hoarsely, as he looked over his shoulder and watched them run away.

"This way!" Francesco cried as he came up beside Dominic and Antonio. Salvatore had run around an olive tree and met them on the other side. The loud insults of the boys echoed after them as they raced out of the orchard. They didn't stop running until they had gone through a field, to the edge of the village.

Once they had come to an old stone barn, the boys sank down in one of the stalls to rest.

"I wonder what happened to the giant," Antonio whispered. "Did you see the way he fell to the ground?"

"Did anyone see him stand up again?" asked Salvatore.

"I didn't turn around to look," Francesco said.

"Do you think he was having a heart attack?" asked Dominic. "Did you see the way he was grabbing his chest?"

"No," Francesco assured him. "I think he was just surprised by what hit him. Although turning the other cheek would have been a far better solution." He glared at Salvatore.

Salvatore looked worried. "I didn't mean to hurt him," he said. "I only threw the manure so he would leave Dominic alone." Then Salvatore looked guiltily at Francesco.

"What's the matter with you?" Francesco asked, giving Salvatore's arm a gentle shove.

Salvatore studied the ground as he whispered, "I dropped the net . . . and then I forgot to pick up the birds . . ."

"What?" Francesco began to shout. "What are you saying? That was our dinner! When are you going to learn to keep your mouth shut?"

"What do you mean?" Salvatore asked. "What did I say?"

"Tu sei un fungo! Tu sei un fungo!" Francesco reminded him, poking him each time he said it. "Why did you have to tell him he was made like a mushroom? If you hadn't insulted the pig boy, he wouldn't have called for the giant."

The thought of Sausage being made like a mushroom suddenly struck Dominic as funny. He began to laugh uncontrollably, and soon the others joined in.

But when the laughter died down, Antonio became serious.

"I'm lucky Dominic was there," he said. He rested his curly blond head against Dominic's arm. His head was warm and moist with the musty smell of little boy sweat.

The boys nodded their heads as Antonio recounted, blow-by-blow, the entire episode of how Dominic heroically saved him from the whip. As Antonio spoke, Dominic remembered the words of the old man back at the museum: "Open your heart, little one. And all that you need shall be yours."

He wasn't sure just what those words meant, but he was sure of one thing. Somehow these boys had opened his heart, had made him care. But to care about someone else, someone he could lose, was as terrifying to Dominic as it was exciting.

As he sat thinking of all this, Francesco grabbed Dominic by the shoulders and pulled him close.

"You took the lash today for my brother," Francesco said. "From this day forward you are family. We shall treat you as one of us."

Dominic felt a lump in his throat. He tried to

talk, but the words wouldn't come. No one in his entire life had ever called him family.

But these boys were different. They genuinely liked him. And Francesco, his favorite, said the words Dominic had waited his whole life to hear:

"You are family."

Dominic let the words play over and over in his mind.

CHAPTER
FIFTEEN

"WE MUST FIND FATHER TOMASO right away,"
Francesco said as he brushed the straw from his
shorts. With all the commotion, they nearly forgot to find out why he had sent Nina after them
with his urgent message.

With an eye to the orchard, the boys made
their way along the old stone wall that wound its
way down the hillside and through the village of
Avaletto.

As they walked, Dominic looked over his
shoulder and listened for the tinkle of donkey
bells. His stinging back made him wary of meeting the giant again.

Violetta trotted up alongside of Dominic, and
she nudged his leg with her nose. He smiled and
reached out to pet her, glad for the chance to take
his mind off his worries.

"Does she really eat anything?" he asked
Francesco as she gently nibbled his fingers.

"She would eat herself to death if she could find enough food," Salvatore quipped before Francesco could answer.

"I never let her graze near poisonous plants," Francesco admitted. "Goats are smarter than most animals except when it comes to food and puddles."

"Puddles?" Dominic asked.

"I have to keep her away from mud and puddles. She gets foot rot if she stands too long in a wet place," Francesco explained. "Haven't you ever cared for animals?"

"No, I've never had the chance," Dominic admitted sadly. "I never lived in one place long enough. But I've had lots of imaginary pets." He went on to tell them about his imaginary dogs and kittens and the monkey he pretended he had.

Antonio's cheeks dimpled as he grinned. "I, too, dream about having a monkey someday."

Soon Dominic found himself telling the boys about the family he wished he had. He had never told anyone about his dream family before, not even his caseworker. He didn't think other people would understand, and he was afraid that they might even laugh at him. But the Candiano brothers had no trouble understanding.

The boys loved hearing Dominic's dream, especially the part about the warm brownies on the kitchen table. But first Dominic had to explain just what a brownie was.

Salvatore told Dominic about his dream family, which consisted of a cowboy father and a mother who made *calamari,* squid, every night for supper.

The thought of having a cowboy father made Dominic smile. But the thought of having squid every night for supper didn't appeal to Dominic at all.

I'd rather have a mother who made pizza, he thought.

Dominic had never felt so content or comfortable trading dreams and stories with people. If only he weren't so hungry, everything would have been perfect.

When they finally reached the cobblestoned *piazza,* the village square, Dominic stood and stared. An ancient stone wall surrounded houses that leaned every which way, higgledy-piggledy, all along the cliff's edge. A jumble of red-tiled roofs dipped and dove as they connected one house to the next. A copper-colored rooster crowed loudly as he perched on a rooftop, while three snowy white hens looked on silently.

In fairy tale fashion, the doorways and shutters of the old houses were splashed with color. Pink and red blossoms spilled over window boxes and balconies everywhere. An old man and a donkey, carrying bundles of twigs, slowly clip-clopped their way down one of the narrow cobbled streets. The air held the scent of wood smoke mixed with the pungent smells of rotting fruit, fresh manure, and the faint fragrance of lemons. Dominic looked down, careful to sidestep the piles of horse manure that were everywhere.

As they continued on, they turned down a winding street. It brought them to a large mulberry tree that grew in the center of a small courtyard. Sitting under the tree was a big burly man plucking feathers from a goose. On seeing the boys, he jumped up, causing a cloud of goose feathers to fall all around him.

The man wore a white apron over his long black robe. A pair of thick leather sandals were strapped to his bare feet. His big, balding head was fringed in dark ringlets, and his round face held the shadow of a day-old beard.

"*Grazie a Dio!* Thanks be to God!" he said, still holding the goose by the crook of its skinny neck. He made the sign of the cross with his free hand.

"You're here at last! I've been looking all over for you."

"I guess you weren't looking in the right places, Father," Antonio chirped.

The priest laughed and ruffled Antonio's blond curls. Dominic could see why the boys loved him so. As big and burly as he was, Father Tomaso was a sweet, gentle man.

Francesco quickly introduced Dominic, but before he could explain his situation, they were interrupted by the priest.

"We have very little time," Father Tomaso said, tossing the goose into the basket by his stool, and pulling off his apron. "Come with me."

They hurried after him into the small stone house that was attached to the church. Francesco crossed himself as they passed a statue that stood in a windowsill. Salvatore and Antonio did the same.

The clip-clopping of Violetta's hooves could be heard on the cool stone floors as she followed them through a small kitchen and into a book-lined study at the rear of the house.

"Shoo, Vito!" the priest said, ushering a rooster out of the room.

"Father, we want to ask you about our friend," Francesco began.

"Certainly, my son," Father Tomaso replied as he rummaged through a pile of papers on his desk. "But first we must attend to this most important matter. Now, where did I put that paper?" A feather fell from his robe as he bent over his desk. "Ah, yes, here we are. This is what I've been looking for!"

He turned and gave the brothers a long, serious look.

"I promised your mama, as she lay dying, with Antonio still a babe in her arms, that I would do what I could to find you a family," he said. "With your papa gone before her and no other family to care for you, she didn't want you running like a pack of wild pups."

Francesco reached up and smoothed down a cowlick on his unbrushed head, while Salvatore pulled Antonio's hand away from a scab that he was picking on his arm. Even Violetta seemed to stifle a burp as she nibbled on the raggedy frayed edges of Francesco's shorts.

"I'm afraid I couldn't keep my promise, until now," the priest continued.

"What do you mean, Father?" Francesco asked.

"Families," Father Tomaso said. "Through the church's orphan fund in America, two families have been found for you. Your ship, the *New Amsterdam*, leaves from Napoli in two days time. I know it is short notice, but the letter was held up in the mail. It only just arrived here yesterday morning from America."

"America!" Salvatore exclaimed. "Father, are you saying that we're to go to America?"

"Yes, my son. I've found two Italian families who will sponsor you. One is in a place called

New Jersey and the other in New York." Father Tomaso smiled uneasily.

"Two families?" Francesco's dark eyebrows furrowed.

"It is not the situation I would have wished for you," Father Tomaso sighed. "But it's the best we can do for now."

"We won't be separated," Francesco said firmly.

"I know you don't want to be apart, but you must be reasonable, Francesco," the priest pleaded. "Who would be able to take in all three of you? That's three extra mouths to feed. We were lucky to find one family from New Jersey who will take two of you in and pay for your passage."

The three brothers stood shaking their heads no.

"If you don't take this opportunity, what will become of you?" Father Tomaso tried to reason with them. "Do you want to sleep on straw and starve for the rest of your lives? In America you can go to school and learn trades."

"Will these families feed us in America?" Antonio asked.

"Yes, little one, they have plenty of food in America."

"It is my dream to go to America one day, Father," Salvatore spoke up. "But not if it means that I must be separated from my brothers."

"Our mama wouldn't have wanted us to be apart," Francesco added.

"Your mama wouldn't have wanted you to be hungry all the time either," Father Tomaso pointed out. "Look at yourselves. Do you really believe that your parents would have wanted this kind of life for you, to be dressed in rags, to be living in a barn, and to be stealing for your every meal?"

"But we are a *famiglia*," Francesco told him. "We stay together. That is what our mama and papa both would have wanted."

"Are you certain of this, my son?" the priest asked gently.

Francesco nodded his head. "Yes, Father, I am certain."

Dominic breathed a sigh of relief, for he didn't know what would become of him if Francesco and the others were to leave him.

Suddenly there came a rapping on the little window behind the desk that startled them all.

Father Tomaso turned around and unlatched the pane.

"Not now, Angelina, I am busy," he called to the little stooped woman in black who waited for him.

"But, Father . . ." the old woman insisted.

"Do not worry, Angelina," Father Tomaso assured her. "I will get you the goose's neck for your pot in a minute."

"It's someone else's neck that you need to be worried about," the old woman replied. "Something bad has happened, Father. You had better come right away."

"All right, all right." Father Tomaso shrugged. "It's probably Spadoni's pig gotten out of his fence again and tearing up her basil. What am I to do about a pig that loves to eat basil?" he grumbled as he hurried out the door. "Stay put. I will be right back."

He did return shortly, but the color had drained from his face.

"What is it, Father?" Salvatore asked, on seeing the priest's stricken look. "Did Spadoni's pig get loose again?"

"No, it's not Spadoni's pig. It's Tibero Randizzi," answered Father Tomaso, his voice full of disbelief. "He's dead, murdered."

"Murdered?" Salvatore gasped.

"Yes, and they say they know who killed him. They're hunting for the murderer right now."

"Who?" Salvatore asked. "Who is the murderer?"

Father Tomaso paused and then in a whisper he said, "It is you, my son. They say you killed Tibero Randizzi!"

CHAPTER SIXTEEN

DOMINIC COULD HARDLY BELIEVE his ears. Salvatore, a murderer? The boys were quick to tell the priest of their incident with Tibero Randizzi earlier that day. They were ashamed to admit that they had been stealing again in the orchard, but they explained how Randizzi had grabbed his chest and fallen before them.

"We had only meant to take enough fruit to satisfy our stomachs," Francesco explained. "We meant no one any harm."

Father Tomaso listened to all they had to say, then he turned to look out the window. Dominic followed his gaze to see old Angelina, wringing her hands and shaking her head as she waited at the window.

Finally Father Tomaso turned back to them and spoke.

"Angelina heard this news as she did her washing at the well. That means the entire village will have heard of it. You haven't much time. You must leave at once."

"But Father, you don't think I am a murderer? Do you?" Salvatore demanded.

"There are a great many things that I do not know." Father Tomaso sighed. "I am but a poor village priest. There is much that escapes me in this big world, but if I know anything it is the hearts of those who kneel in my church.

"I have known you boys since you wore your baby dresses. I dipped your heads in the holy water. I know you are not murderers, but I also know the wrath of the *padrone*. He is a vindictive man and there will be no reasoning with him. If his son has accused you of this crime and has others to verify his story, you are in grave danger. He will want an eye for an eye."

"But if Salvatore gets a good lawyer he will get off," Dominic said, thinking of all the courtroom dramas he had watched on television.

"The *padrone* is all the law that rules in this village," Father Tomaso interrupted. "We cannot risk Salvatore's life. They could throw him into a prison down in Napoli and he would never live to see sunlight again."

The priest's face suddenly brightened. "Unless he were to go to Napoli himself. The ship that I told you about is waiting in the harbor as we speak. Thankfully these tickets only just arrived, and I haven't had the chance to tell anyone else about them. You'd all be safe in America, Francesco, and your brothers would have a good life there."

Dominic watched as Francesco's eyes filled with tears.

"How?" he asked. "How would they separate us?"

The room grew suddenly still as they all waited for Father Tomaso's answer.

"The two youngest, Antonio and Salvatore, are to go to New Jersey. And Francesco, they've found a family for you in New York. They've even found work for you already, building roads. It's a great opportunity."

"I don't want to live away from Francesco!" Antonio cried.

"You must be brave, Antonio," Father Tomaso said, placing his big hand on Antonio's mop of golden curls. "These two places, New York and New Jersey, are not a great distance apart. Francesco can visit you. Your brother is doing what is best for all of you. You must be brave.

"And you best leave now, so you can make it to the harbor by tomorrow morning," Father Tomaso continued as he searched his desk for a pen and paper. "Stay off the main road and keep well hidden. I will stay here and try to divert them. But how? Ah!" he cried, clapping his hands. "Mention Rome to me," he suddenly demanded.

"What?" Francesco asked.

"Rome, Rome!" Father Tomaso cried. "Mention Rome!"

"Rome?"

"*Molto bene!* Very good!" the priest cried. "I will tell them that I saw you and yes, you mentioned Rome. Always best to have the truth on your side." His eyes twinkled as he smiled. "*Se Dio vuole,* God willing, I will meet up with you in Napoli tomorrow."

He picked up his pen and began to write. "Go to the chest, Francesco," he ordered, without looking up, "and take your shoes and good shirts. You will need them for the journey. It's lucky that you left them here for Mass and not in the barn. They're sure to be looking for you there. Oh, and take your mama's rosary beads as well."

Francesco lifted a little wooden chest by the door, and pulled out a strand of worn wooden rosary beads, a pair of old leather shoes, and an empty cloth sack. He reached back into the chest, pulling out three folded shirts, and quickly threw them into the sack.

"Once you reach Napoli, find Pasquale, the clam seller," Father Tomaso instructed, getting to his feet. "He has his stall on the corner of the Via Roma. Tell him that I sent you and he will direct you to my sister, Signora Giasullo's house. Give her this letter." He handed an envelope to Francesco. "My sister and her husband will take you in for the night."

"*Grazie,* Father, thank you," Francesco whispered.

"Ah, Francesco." The good priest sighed, coming around the desk and hugging him hard. "Look after your brothers. They are good boys. You are all good boys. Oh, you've slipped now and then with your thievery and your wild ways, but deep down there is more goodness than devilry there. I know you will grow to be great men in America. Avaletto will miss you. I will miss you. If all goes well, I will see you off at the boat. Go now, my sons."

As he hugged Father Tomaso, Francesco caught sight of Dominic standing all alone.

"Father," he whispered turning back to the priest. "Our friend here was caught in the earthquake down south. He's become a brother to us. Please, Father, can you find him a way to America, too?"

"I'm afraid there is only passage for three," Father Tomaso replied, shaking his head. "It has taken me over four years to secure you such generous sponsors. But I shall see what I can do. And maybe some day, your friend will be as lucky as you three."

For the first time since he had met the brothers, Dominic felt alone. What was to become of him by himself in this strange time and place?

"At least come with us as far as the harbor," Salvatore begged. Dominic nodded his head yes. He was too upset to speak.

Antonio clasped Dominic's hands in his and looked up at him sadly.

"I wish you could come with us," he said.

"He's so confused from the earthquake, Father," Francesco whispered. "I don't think he should be alone."

"Maybe Pasquale, the clam seller, can find work for him on the streets," Father Tomaso suggested. "After that, we shall have to see what happens."

Dominic nodded, and bit down on his lip. He was accustomed to living from day to day and "seeing what happens." It was how he had lived his whole life. But how could he trust his life to "what happens" in a strange country almost one hundred years back in time?

As fearful as he was, he was also overcome with sadness. For the first time in his life Dominic Cantori had found a family he cared about, and who cared about him.

Even though the Candiano brothers weren't

like his dream family, with a mother and a father, and brothers and sisters, and a nice house, and a sheep dog, these three brothers living in a barn with their goat were the best friends he had ever known. And now he was about to lose them, too.

CHAPTER SEVENTEEN

As THEY MADE THEIR WAY down the hillside, the four boys kept a sharp lookout for the *padrone's* search party. They hoped that Father Tomaso's "mention" of the north had worked, but they were still careful to stay well out of sight.

After walking for what seemed like hours they agreed to stop for a rest.

"Shh . . . listen," Francesco whispered. "You can still hear the bells."

Dominic listened and he could just make out the faint ringing of bells in the distance.

"We've never lived beyond the sound of the bell tower," Francesco said sadly. "It will seem very strange not to hear them."

"Maybe they will have a bell tower in New York," Antonio suggested. They all grew quiet again, listening for the familiar ringing.

"I wonder how many men it will take to bury him," Salvatore said, suddenly.

"Who?" Antonio asked.

"Randizzi, of course," Salvatore answered. "They're going to need a giant casket to hold him."

Francesco nodded his head as he took the cloth sack off his back. Antonio pulled out the shoes and put them on.

"They look awfully big for your little feet," Dominic couldn't help but notice.

Antonio frowned. "They were Papa's shoes," he said.

"They fit me best," Francesco admitted. "But we take turns wearing them for Mass and on feast days."

"Salvatore and I have to stuff them with rags to make them fit," Antonio explained. "Can I wear them now?" he asked his brother. "Now that we're going to America."

"No, you haven't any rags to stuff them with here, and it's too far a walk yet," Francesco told him. "I'll carry them in my pack and when we reach America you can put them on."

"Why does he get to wear them and not me?" Salvatore snapped, pounding his chest with his fist and pulling one of the shoes off of Antonio's foot.

"Your feet smell worse than mine," Antonio retorted as he tried to get the shoe back.

"Stop it, you two!" Francesco ordered. "How many times must I tell you about sharing? Now why can't you figure this out for yourselves."

"I can figure it out," Antonio bragged. "I'll wear this shoe and he can wear that one."

Dominic grinned and Francesco shook his head.

"As ridiculous as two donkeys trying to pull a cart from both ends." Francesco sighed. "What will you do when you get to America and you don't have me to settle your squabbles?"

This last question hung in the air like a heavy cloud.

"What *will* we do without you, Francesco?" Antonio whimpered.

But Francesco got hold of himself quickly.

"You will do your best to remember that no matter where we go, we are always a family. This is not the end of the Candianos." He smiled. "It is just the beginning of the Candianos in America. We'll be a family there too, I promise."

Everyone seemed to brighten at this thought, and they once again set off on the paths down the hillside.

Antonio did his best to keep up with Salvatore, who was practically running. He was so anxious to see the ship. It was only Francesco who kept stopping and turning around, keeping a constant watch for the *padrone's* men.

With the village finally out of sight, and the bells out of earshot, Francesco began talking to Violetta, who would often comment with a nod of her head or a blink of her eye.

"I wonder what the journey on the ship will be like," Salvatore said excitedly.

"I hope Violetta doesn't get seasick," Francesco worried. "She's never been out at sea before."

"Neither have we," Salvatore exclaimed.

"You're not as sensitive as a goat," Francesco told him.

"No one is as sensitive as your Violetta," Salvatore quipped.

Dominic understood Francesco's concern. If he had Violetta for a pet, he would have felt the same way.

With the crimson sun sinking low behind a line of cedar trees, Francesco decided they had best make camp for the night.

"It's no more than a two hour's walk from here to the harbor," he said. "But I don't want to get to the city at nightfall. The streets are known to be dangerous after dark. There are thieves and cutthroats about then. So we'll sleep here and leave at first light tomorrow."

With all the fresh air and the excitement they had had that day, Dominic's hunger was growing worse. No one else mentioned food or the lack of it. Dominic guessed that they were used to going to bed hungry.

They made a soft bed of pine needles, and everyone lay down. As the sky filled with stars and a silvery moon hung above them, they talked in hushed whispers about the journey they were about to make.

"I wonder if there are stars in the sky over America," Antonio murmured.

"It's not another planet," Dominic said. "Of course there are stars in the sky. But sometimes you can't see them because of the pollution from the cars and the light from the sodium lamps."

"Pollution? Cars? Sodium lamps? What are they?" Francesco asked.

Dominic hesitated, not knowing how to answer. "You see in the America I know, there are lots of cars that you ride around in, but no horses."

"Horseless carriages?" Salvatore asked. "We've heard of them."

"Yes, well in the America I know everyone has one and they make the air very dirty. And the sodium lamps are bright orange lights that they use at night to control crime."

Everyone grew quiet at this remark.

"What else do you know of America?" Salvatore demanded.

Dominic hesitated, not knowing how to answer. "Well, I guess I know a lot," he finally admitted.

"Maybe he had relatives who went there before the earthquake," Francesco whispered furtively to Salvatore. "That's probably how he knows so much. He's got it mixed up in his mind that he was there himself."

"Nello Poloni's cousin told us the streets of America are paved with gold," Antonio said. "But Emmalina's uncles went there and didn't find any."

"Emmalina thought that maybe they were looking on the wrong streets," Salvatore continued. "But then they wrote to her mother to say there was only horse manure on the streets, like here.

"So, which is it?" Salvatore asked. "Gold or manure?"

CHAPTER
EIGHTEEN

"GOLD OR MANURE?" Dominic repeated the words aloud as he scratched his head. "Actually, there's neither. Not in the America I know. Sometimes you can find money on the streets, but not very much. Some people can get rich if they work hard. But others work hard and never get rich."

"I'd be glad to have the chance to work for some gold," Salvatore said. "I want to work as a cowboy."

"Do you know a lot about cowboys?" Dominic asked.

"Salvatore knows all about them," Antonio assured him.

"Angelo Foretta's uncle showed me pictures of them," Salvatore said proudly. "They were wearing big white hats and they had shiny guns and silver spurs."

"He talks of nothing else since he's seen them," Francesco muttered.

"I will come and visit you, Francesco, in New York City," Salvatore promised. "I will get a job and buy us each a gun and a horse and we can ride over to see you. Then we can sit under the stars at night and eat linguini together."

Dominic closed his eyes and tried to imagine the cowboys he remembered from old western movies. "You know, I don't think cowboys ate linguini under the stars," he said.

"No?" Salvatore looked surprised. "Then what do they eat? Pizza?"

"Well, I don't think cowboys ate pizza, either," Dominic said.

"What then?" Antonio asked.

"Beans, I guess. Lots of beans," Dominic told them. "I think it's going to be different from what you're expecting."

"I'm expecting to see those big hairy buffalos," Salvatore informed him.

Dominic grinned and reached into his pants pocket. He pulled out a half dozen pebbles, before pulling out his nickel. It was the old Indian head nickel that he had found on Ninth Street, back home in Brooklyn. He held it out to Salvatore now.

"What coin is this?" Salvatore asked, turning the nickel over in his hand.

"It's an American Indian head nickel," Dominic told him. "And on the other side is a buffalo."

Salvatore sighed with envy. "I cannot understand the words, but I can see it is a buffalo. I wish I had one," he said, tracing it lovingly with his finger.

"It's a pretty rare nickel," Dominic bragged. "Not a lot of kids have one."

"You are so lucky to have such a coin," Salvatore whispered. "I wish I had something good enough to trade for it."

"Oh, I would never trade anything for it," Dominic told him. "I just thought you'd like to see it."

Dominic took a deep breath of the tangy pine-scented air and he couldn't help smiling over Salvatore's envy.

He took the nickel back and held it in his hand. Then his eyes widened as Dominic noticed the date on the face of the coin.

"Look!" he cried. "The date on my nickel. I almost forgot about it. It's 1936. This is proof that what I said was true. I'm from the future."

Salvatore and the others peered down at the date on the coin, but they were not impressed.

"It's all in English." Francesco shrugged. "How do we know what those numbers mean? It could be the date or maybe just the number of the coin."

Dominic put the nickel back in his pocket. He knew it was useless to try to convince them.

"What else do you know about cowboys?" Salvatore asked.

"Let's see," Dominic said. "I learned 'Home on the Range' a long time ago, and that's a real cowboy song."

"Teach us! Teach us!" Salvatore and Antonio exclaimed at once. "We want to learn to sing like real American cowboys." Even Francesco seemed interested, although he warned them to keep their voices low.

"Okay." Dominic laughed. He remembered how bored the boys in his music class were when their teacher, Miss Felkner, tried to teach them the song. Dominic concentrated now, as he worked hard to remember the first verse.

Awed into silence, the Candiano boys hung onto every word he sang. And soon the still night air was filled with the perfect harmony of their voices, singing just above a whisper. As the stars grew bright overhead, Francesco and Antonio were quick to fall asleep. But Dominic and Salvatore stayed awake, and they talked late into the night.

"You know, Dominic," Salvatore whispered. "I hope to be like you someday."

"Me?" Dominic said.

"Sure. You are brave and kind and you know

real American cowboy songs." He ducked his head shyly. "You are my hero."

"I like you, too, Salvatore," Dominic finally managed to whisper awkwardly. Looking at the stars overhead, the two boys talked about heroes and cowboys until they grew so tired, they couldn't talk anymore. It was a night Dominic knew he would always remember. He didn't want it to end.

When Dominic finally closed his eyes, he was lulled by the voice of Salvatore, who softly sang:

> *"Where seldom is heard*
> *a discouraging word*
> *and the skies are not cloudy all day . . ."*

CHAPTER NINETEEN

SALVATORE'S VOICE was the last thing Dominic heard before falling asleep that night, and it was the first thing he heard the next morning. But this time Salvatore was not singing. He was groaning.

"My stomach hurts," he cried.

Dominic sat up to find Salvatore doubled over in pain, clutching his belly.

"I told you not to swallow all those cherry pits yesterday," Francesco scolded. "Antonio, what are you doing?" he called. Antonio had knelt beside Salvatore and was trying to look up his nose.

"I think I see the tree starting to grow," Antonio whispered.

While Dominic and Francesco laughed, Salvatore groaned and pushed Antonio away.

"Are you feeling good enough to walk?" Francesco asked, putting his arm on his brother's shoulder. "We must reach the city today."

Salvatore's face was white. He bit down on his lower lip to quell the pain, but he insisted he could walk. They were still over an hour away from the harbor. It was an easy walk going down the well-worn path, but they had to stop several times as Salvatore was doubled over in pain.

Francesco frowned. "It's not good to travel with a sour stomach," he said.

"I can make it. I can make it," Salvatore insisted. Dominic and Francesco took turns helping him to walk.

They continued down until they finally reached the cobbled streets of the city. Dominic was glad to be off the stony hillside. He was not used to walking barefoot, and his tender feet were now quite bruised. Suddenly the little group found themselves walking into a fantasia of color, voices, and music.

"*Vide Napoli e poi morì*. See Naples and then die," Francesco whispered.

"What are you talking about?" Dominic asked nervously.

"It's an old saying," Francesco explained. "They say you haven't lived until you've seen this city."

I just hope I can find a way to stay alive in this city, Dominic thought. He stared at the women in long skirts and the men in cloth caps as they swarmed along the side streets that climbed toward the higher quarters of the city. Fountains gurgled, a baby cried, and a young girl hung over a balcony, singing to the passersby below.

All the activity reminded him of the hustle and bustle of his streets back home in Brooklyn. But the look and smell of this place were quite different. Great domed buildings with ornate stone carvings rose up above the terra-cotta-colored roofs. The strong scent of ripe hay and manure was thick in the sea air, along with the pungent aroma of seaweed and fish. Shifty-eyed con men stood on street corners hawking their goods to the wary immigrants about to embark.

"Teeth pulled!" one shouted, grabbing hold of Dominic's arm. "Don't make the voyage with a mouth full of rotten teeth."

Dominic squirmed his way out of the man's grip and broke into a run to catch up with Francesco and the others.

"Authentic American shirts," wailed another after them.

"Don't arrive in America looking like a greenhorn."

"Relics of the saints to calm an angry ocean," promised another.

"Hair from the head of Saint Christopher, guaranteed to secure a safe journey."

"We have no money," Francesco told them. "Only our tickets."

"Why did you tell them that?" Dominic whispered frantically to Francesco. "You never tell someone on the street what you've got on you." But Francesco didn't seem to understand, and Dominic soon realized that coming from a little mountain village, Francesco was not as street smart as a person coming from a place like Brooklyn.

Dominic felt something brush against his sleeve and he turned to see a grimy-faced boy, younger than himself, trying to pick his pocket. He pushed him away, then another smaller boy slipped his hand into Francesco's backpack.

"Hey!" Francesco yelled. "Stop! He's stolen our shoes!"

CHAPTER TWENTY

DOMINIC AND FRANCESCO chased after the thief, with Salvatore, Antonio, and Violetta lagging behind. They ran past a crippled woman, who sat cackling on a stoop, past the sound of mandolin music that beckoned from a darkened doorway, past a band of dirty-faced boys dressed in rags, who laughed as they knelt over a card game in a grimy alleyway. But it was no use. The thief had vanished.

"He was probably after the tickets," Dominic gasped as they caught their breath in a doorway, finally giving up the chase.

Francesco pulled the tickets out from the sack and smiled. But looking down at his dirty stained feet, his smile quickly faded.

"Now we'll have no shoes to wear in America," he cried, pounding his fist against a building.

Salvatore and Antonio looked down at their bare feet and frowned.

"What about our shirts and Mama's rosary beads?" Salvatore asked.

"They are safe," Francesco declared. "And they'll have to fight us to the ground before they'll get those."

Salvatore began to complain again about his stomachache as he reached for Antonio's hand.

"Maybe he should see a doctor," Dominic suggested.

"A doctor?" Salvatore looked alarmed.

"We've never been to a doctor," Francesco explained. "No, what Salvatore needs is to lie still. Once we get to Signora Giasullo's house, he'll be able to rest. All we have to do is to find the clam seller."

He turned toward Violetta. "Stay close to me," Francesco whispered, placing a short rope around her neck. She was quick to answer with an uneasy bleat.

Together the little group cautiously walked down a narrow, crowded street, under a great canopy of dripping laundry, and past a shuttered window, from which the woeful lament of a concertina drifted.

They walked through alleyways, down winding streets, and past courtyards, asking for directions and looking for the street corner as Father Tomaso had directed them. Francesco let out a sigh of relief as they spotted a small wooden cart standing at the corner of a busy street.

A dark-skinned boy in an old, stained sailor's shirt was reaching into a barrel of fish. Francesco walked up to him and smiled.

"*Buon giorno.* Good day. Is this the Via Roma?" Francesco asked.

"Yes."

"And are you Pasquale?"

"Who wants to know?" the boy snapped with a suspicious glint in his eyes.

When Francesco mentioned Father Tomaso the boy looked up from his fish and grinned. Dominic noticed that many of his teeth were stained and rotted.

"Yes, I'm Pasquale," he admitted. "And Father Tomaso has been a good friend to me. If you are a friend of his, then I shall treat you in kind."

He quickly agreed to show them to Father Tomaso's sister's house. But first he insisted on giving them something to take along for their evening meal. Dominic tried not to get his hopes up. What he wanted more than anything was a shake, double fries, and a burger to go. His mouth watered at the thought of it.

Still grinning his toothy grin, Pasquale reached into the barrel before him. Dominic felt his stomach lurch at the sight of the rubbery white creature in his hand. It had a head and a tangle of tentacles attached to it.

"*Polpo!* Octopus!" Antonio cried, jumping up and down and clapping his hands. "For us?"

"It's your lucky day," Pasquale said, shaking the wet rubbery mass in the air. "It's all for you. Signora Giasullo is an excellent cook," he said, wrapping a piece of paper around it. "Take it with you and tell her I bit the heart out myself."

"Bit the heart out?" Dominic asked.

"Sure, that's the fastest way to kill them," Pasquale said, clicking his teeth. "One quick bite into the heart."

Dominic gulped and turned his head in disgust, only to see Violetta peering into the barrel, looking for something to eat. She finally decided to eat the barrel instead and tried to nibble its side.

"Good choice," Dominic said under his breath as he pulled her toward him.

"Don't look so worried, my friend," Pasquale said, patting Dominic on the back with his dripping hand. "You'll get a mouthful. She's a big one and only out of the net an hour ago."

A shake, double fries, and eight legs to go, Dominic thought as he smiled at his private joke.

"Yes, she was an easy catch," Pasquale continued. "One look in the glass and she kissed herself good-bye."

"Glass?" Dominic asked.

"The glass. The mirror. It's how we catch them," Pasquale explained. "We send a mirror down on a line. An octopus becomes so fascinated by its own image that it forgets to swim away. Lucky for you she was so in love with herself. You will go to sleep with full bellies tonight."

Dominic gulped again, Antonio and Francesco grinned, and Violetta nodded her head. It was only Salvatore who did not seem interested at all. He had slumped against a wall and was holding his side.

"Your friend there does not look well," Pasquale said. When Francesco told him about Salvatore's eating all the cherry pits, the clam seller shook his head and reached into his back pocket.

"I usually sell these for more than my fish," he said, pulling a little dirty cloth bag out of his pocket. "But because you are friends of Father Tomaso, I will give you a few for free, no charge."

"What are they?" Antonio asked, standing on tiptoes to see.

"Relics," he whispered, pulling three yellowed fingernails out of the bag, and handing them to Salvatore. "These are the fingernails of Saint Sebastian. They are able to cure a sour stomach, a blow to the head, poor eyesight, and nosebleeds.

Just carry these relics in your pocket and you will be cured."

"*Grazie*, Pasquale. Thank you," Francesco said. Then he asked him if he knew of their ship, the *New Amsterdam*.

"I know all the ships that come into the harbor," Pasquale assured him.

"Umberto," he called to a skinny, dirty-faced boy drinking at a fountain. "Come watch my stand for me." The boy came and stood beside the barrel with a hopeful look in his eye.

"And don't let me catch you eating my clams," Pasquale shouted. "Come," he said, turning back to the boys. "We'll go to see your ship. It's just past the old cobbler's shop down at the bay. Come, I know a shortcut."

They followed Pasquale down an alley when Salvatore suddenly cried out.

"Salvatore, are you all right?" Francesco called, running to his brother.

"It's my side," Salvatore groaned. "It's worse. It's worse . . ." his voice trailed off, as he closed his eyes. "I can't walk."

"You can't take him to the ship like this," Pasquale whispered. "They won't let him board if he's sick. He'll have to get better first."

"But our tickets are only good for tomorrow. We must leave tomorrow," Francesco cried.

"Come, we'll carry him the rest of the way," Pasquale offered. "Maybe the relics will fix his stomach in time."

Francesco handed Violetta's rope to Dominic, while he and Pasquale took turns carrying Salvatore piggyback, down the street. By the time they had reached a heavy wooden doorway, Salvatore's face was covered in sweat, and he was burning with fever.

An old woman in a black dress and a lace shawl greeted them at the door. It was Signora Giasullo. She smiled on seeing Pasquale, but her round face became creased with worry at the sight of Salvatore's condition.

Francesco gave her the letter as Father Tomaso had instructed, and she quickly read it.

"Ah, yes, I met your mama long ago," she said. "When I came up to visit my brother, I would see her at the well doing her wash or in church saying the Novenas. A good woman, your mama."

"Agh!" Salvatore cried out in pain.

Signora Giasullo ordered Salvatore to be brought to her bed and called to her sisters-in-law across the street to come at once.

As the women swarmed into the cramped dwelling to attend to the patient, there was little room for anyone else. Dominic and the others followed one of the women through the house and out to a small courtyard, where they found a table and chairs under an arbor covered in grape vines. Dominic could hear the low buzzing of bees above their heads as he sat in one of the chairs.

The woman placed a bowl of blue grapes on the table

"*Mangiate!* Eat!" she told them. They quickly emptied the bowl.

"It's all my fault," Francesco moaned, as he fed a grape to Violetta. "I should have made him spit out those pits."

"Do you think that the cherry tree is going to grow so big that it will burst his stomach?" Antonio whispered anxiously.

"No, Antonio, stomachs are no place for trees," Dominic told him. "They can't really grow in there."

"But maybe all those pits can burst a stomach," Francesco said.

"Will they let you into America with a burst stomach?" Antonio asked. No one answered this last question for Signora Giasullo was calling from the window. They jumped up and ran inside.

"This child is very sick," she whispered, shaking her head. "I don't know how he can make such a journey."

"He has to try," Francesco insisted. He told her about the cherry pits and she frowned.

"Ah, well we shall see," she finally whispered.

The boys stayed with Salvatore, and Violetta lay down beside the bed.

"What's wrong with her?" Dominic asked, noticing how listless she was.

"She knows Salvatore is ill," Francesco explained. "Whenever one of us takes ill, Violetta knows and she worries."

Dominic looked down at Violetta's dark, sad eyes and he patted her head. "Don't worry, Violetta," he whispered.

But after a few hours had passed, and Salvatore's condition had not improved, they all began to worry.

"Come, take a meal with us," Signora Giasullo insisted, leading them back out to the table under the arbor.

A meal of octopus, Dominic thought grimly, following the others back to the table. A kind-faced man with a thick red mustache introduced himself as Signor Giasullo and sat down at the head of the table with them to eat. Dominic watched as everyone made the sign of the cross and lowered their heads to pray. Signor Giasullo led the prayer and when he was through, he picked up a knife and kissed it before slicing into a loaf of warm homemade bread.

The boys all sat silently eyeing the plates of delicious-smelling food that two young girls were placing on the table. There was a basket of warm bread and two wooden bowls full of greens and roasted peppers. There was not much to go around, but what was there was meant to be shared by all.

Dominic kept his eye out for the octopus as he picked up a wooden spoon by his plate. Francesco passed him a large bowl full of a spicy tomato sauce with bits of what Dominic guessed were chicken pieces in it.

"This smells good," he said, passing Antonio the bowl.

"*Zuppa di polpo* always smells good," replied Antonio with a grin. "Stewed octopus always smells good."

Dominic dipped his spoon into the thick red sauce. He gulped down one mouthful and then another. Soon he had forgotten all about the rubbery mass of tentacles that Pasquale had pulled from his bucket. Soon all he could think of was how delicious octopus tasted!

Father Tomaso arrived a little before sunset, having come down from the hills on his donkey, Piccolo. He told them that all had gone as he hoped, with the *padrone's* men off searching to the north.

"But when they find no trace of you there, they are sure to come south to the harbor to look," Father Tomaso told them. "Whatever you do, Francesco, you must get on that ship tomorrow."

Later that night they went in to see Salvatore, but he was too sick to talk. His shirt was wet with sweat, and Signora Giasullo was helping him out of it. As Dominic stood beside the bed, he noticed that Salvatore wore a chain around his neck. Dominic took a step closer to the bed, and in the light of the lamp he saw something that surprised him. For there, hanging from the end of the chain on his neck, was a familiar little gold key!

CHAPTER TWENTY-ONE

DOMINIC WAS TOO STUNNED TO TALK. As he leaned forward to have a closer look, he saw the initials, S.C., scratched on the key. They were scratched in just the same way as the ones on his own lucky key. Before he could say anything, the Signora hurried them out of the room, whispering that Salvatore needed his rest.

Dominic and Antonio followed Francesco as he carried Violetta up the wooden ladder to the attic. That was where Signor Giasullo had laid down featherbeds on the floorboards for them.

All the while Dominic stood clutching his bare neck, trying to make sense of what he had just seen.

"Francesco," he finally whispered. "Where did Salvatore get the key he's wearing around his neck?"

Francesco shrugged. "He found that key last year in the churchyard. He keeps hoping that a pirate had buried treasure there, and that one day he will find the treasure chest that the key will open."

"What about the initials?"

"Initials?"

"On the key!" Dominic exclaimed. "The initials S.C. How did they get there?" His voice had risen to a cry.

"Calm down, it's only an old key."

"Just tell me about the initials," Dominic pleaded.

"He scratched his initials on the key with Father Tomaso's pin," Antonio explained. "The one he uses for the altar cloth. But don't tell Father."

"S.C.," Dominic whispered. "Salvatore Candiano!"

"Who else would it be?" Francesco replied.

That night Dominic stayed awake long after the others had fallen asleep. He was thinking about his own father's name, Sal. He had never thought that it might be short for something, Salvatore, say. And what would it mean if his father and Salvatore had the same first name?

There was so much that he didn't understand. How did he get Salvatore's key? How did he get here in the first place? Who was the old man on the phone in the museum?

And now there was no time left to figure it all out before the other boys left for America.

CHAPTER
TWENTY-TWO

IN THE MIDDLE OF THE NIGHT, Dominic and
Francesco were suddenly awakened by the sound
of heavy footsteps on the ladder leading to the
loft where they slept.

"Francesco, come," Father Tomaso whispered
in the darkness as the light from his lamp lit his
worried face. "It's Salvatore. He's worse."

They quickly awakened Antonio, and the three
hurried down the ladder. They found Salvatore
lying in the bedroom, groaning and doubled over
with pain. Chalky white and drenched with
sweat, he didn't even notice that they had entered
the room. Signora Giasullo sat by his side, softly
praying and fingering her rosary beads.

"Vittorio, take the little one out to the court-
yard for a drink," Signora Giasullo whispered to
her husband as she guided them all back into the
hallway. Antonio began to protest that he wanted
to stay, but the sadness in the old woman's eyes

quieted him with one glance, and he hurried after Signor Giasullo.

"What is it, Signora?" Francesco whispered. "He'll be well enough to travel by morning, won't he?"

The old woman shook her head.

"But the saint's relics, they'll bring down the fever. Salvatore will get better. He has to get better today," insisted Francesco, clutching her arm.

"He's so very sick," she whispered. "The fever is too high."

"Salvatore has said his prayers and received his last rites," Father Tomaso whispered, placing a hand on Francesco's shoulder.

"No, Father!" Francesco cried. "Don't say that. He's going to get well. He's got to. He's got to get to America so he can be a cowboy. . . ." his words trailed off into a sob.

"You must be strong, Francesco, for Antonio," urged Father Tomaso. "Go to him now. He would want you beside him."

Francesco followed Father Tomaso to the bed. Dominic stared from the doorway, unable to comprehend what he was hearing. How could Salvatore, who was so strong and alive, be dying from a simple stomachache? Salvatore was too young to die. It wasn't possible. It wasn't fair.

"Can't you call an ambulance?" Dominic whispered.

Signora Giasullo looked puzzled and Dominic realized that there were probably none around.

"What about a hospital? Isn't there a hospital we can take him to?"

The old woman sighed. "The malaria has killed so many there. He is better off here."

Francesco looked at Dominic, his dark eyes heavy with sadness.

"He's asking to see you," Francesco said.

Dominic walked to Salvatore's bedside, where he found Salvatore lying, his eyes half closed. His face was flushed with fever and his forehead beaded with sweat. Francesco gently laid a hand on his brother's cheek, and whispered into his ear.

"Hey, cowboy, what are you doing just lying there? You should be up practicing your rope tricks."

Salvatore grimaced. "Francesco, I'm afraid," he gasped.

Dominic could see the pain in his eyes as he struggled to speak.

"Don't be afraid, Salvatore," Francesco said firmly. "You will get better. You will. And we'll get you on the boat to America, tomorrow. I promise."

Salvatore closed his eyes and shook his head. "That's not what I'm worried about. I'm afraid. I'm so afraid . . ."

"Don't worry," Dominic tried to assure him.

"You're going to get well and be a cowboy in America."

"No, it's not that." Salvatore sighed. "Come closer."

Dominic leaned over the bed with his ear to Salvatore's pale lips. "It's horses," Salvatore gasped.

"Horses?"

"Yes, horses. I'm afraid of horses," Salvatore admitted in a weak whisper. "We never could afford one. I've never been able to ride a full-sized horse. How can I be a cowboy if I am afraid of my horse?"

Salvatore groaned, but his eyes were fixed on Dominic.

"Well . . ." Dominic hesitated, trying desperately to comfort his friend. "I don't think you have to worry too much about that."

"No?" Salvatore whispered.

"No," Dominic told him. "Because I think once a cowboy meets his horse, it's like meeting your best friend. You recognize one another right away and know just what to do."

"I hope he recognizes me," Salvatore said, struggling to get the words out. The pain overtook him and he groaned loudly.

"He will," Dominic assured him. "You'll be a great cowboy, with a great horse, and your lucky buffalo nickel."

Dominic reached into his pocket and pulled out his nickel. He felt sorry he hadn't given it to Salvatore sooner. Dominic pressed it into his palm now as a faint smile crept onto Salvatore's face and his eyes began to close.

"That's right, you get some rest now," Dominic whispered. "If you're going to be a cowboy, you've got to get plenty of sleep."

"Francesco," Salvatore called to his brother. "Do you hear?"

Francesco leaned over the bed. "Hear? What do you hear?"

"The bells," Salvatore whispered, his eyes closing. "Don't you hear the bells?" Salvatore gave out a final gasp. His eyes flashed open for a second, and then quickly closed.

"Salvatore!" Francesco cried. "Don't! Please don't go!" He lowered his face onto his brother's chest and began to sob. Dominic stood staring at the old buffalo nickel that had fallen from Salvatore's limp hand onto the faded featherbed.

"Can you hear me, Salvatore? Open your eyes. Please open your eyes," Francesco begged. Violetta nuzzled her way into his lap to comfort him.

"Oh, my sweet," Signora Giasullo whispered, placing her hand on Francesco's shoulder. "He no longer hears. . . ."

Dominic closed his eyes tight, fighting back the cry that was building up inside of him.

And as he listened to Francesco's muffled sobs and the Signora's whispered prayers, he suddenly heard a melody coming from out in the court-yard. Dominic recognized the tune at once. A tear rolled down his cheek as he heard Antonio's con-certina begin to play:

Home, home on the range . . .

CHAPTER TWENTY-THREE

SIGNORA GIASULLO SAT at Salvatore's bedside chanting and wailing as was the custom in that city when someone died. Dominic was glad that he could leave the room. He had never seen anyone die before, except on TV, and when a person died on TV the body didn't stay around. A hearse usually came and it was whisked away out of sight. But no one came for Salvatore. He was still lying on the bed.

Dominic didn't like the wailing. It sounded too sad and scary. He wanted to get as far away from it as he could. He followed Francesco up to the loft, where Antonio had hidden himself under a quilt.

Father Tomaso climbed the wooden ladder after them and sank down on a rickety old chair. "You must not wait for the burial," he said. "The ship leaves at noon."

"I don't want to go without . . ." Francesco's voice choked with a sob.

"I know it is hard, Francesco," Father Tomaso said gently. "But you must think of yourself and your little brother. Maybe if Salvatore had been in America, there would have been a doctor and medicine to save him. In America he wouldn't have had to fill his empty stomach with cherry pits. In America you have a chance for a better life.

"Besides, the *padrone* and his men will surely find you if you stay. With Salvatore gone, they may blame you for Tibero Randizzi's death. You must go. But do not worry. I will see that Salvatore is laid beside your mama and papa, back in Avaletto. I promise you this."

"I want Salvatore," Antonio sobbed from under the quilt.

"Salvatore is in heaven with Mama and Papa now," Francesco told him.

"When can I go to heaven to be with them?" Antonio asked, poking his head out from under the blanket.

"Ah, little one, such a question." Father Tomaso sighed, scooping up Antonio and the quilt in his big, strong arms, and placing him on his lap. "It is not for us to say when our time on earth is through. This is not for us to decide. It is God who makes these decisions."

"But what if God makes mistakes?" Antonio whispered. "How do we know that he meant to take Salvatore?"

"That is what faith is all about," Father Tomaso replied. "Everything happens for the best reasons, reasons that we know little about. Believing in the best is believing in God's goodness. Your mama had great faith."

"But the best doesn't always happen," Dominic blurted out. Everyone turned to look at him and he felt his cheeks burning with embarrassment at the sudden attention.

"Yes, this is true. Good things don't always happen." Father Tomaso nodded. He gently lay Antonio down. Then he walked over to the little crooked window on the far wall. He held back the frayed bit of curtain that hung over the frame. Dominic took a deep breath as the faint scent of lemons blew into the loft on the night's breeze.

"Look at those distant hills in the moonlight," the priest sighed. "Our whole world, our life, is very much like that little patch of hillside you boys have lived on. There are beautiful flowers, and olives, and lemons. But there are bad things too, weeds that choke the flowers, worms that infest the fruit. Good and bad, side by side. Flowers blooming and fading, leaves twirling up to the sun, and fruit rotting on the vine. It goes on and on, changing all the time. One day you will be able to look at everything and discover strength and goodness in the most difficult of changes. For it is the hardships we meet in life that make us strong. And it is our strength that makes us who we are."

"Oh, poor child, he is gone, he is gone," the women's cries could be heard from below, causing Antonio to bury his head back under the quilt. Again, Dominic fought the tears that were coming to his eyes.

"Now you had better get some rest," whispered Father Tomaso, "You will need all your strength for your trip."

As Dominic lay down beside Antonio, Father Tomaso walked over to Francesco. The two of them stood by the moonlit window, where they whispered until the priest turned down the lantern and sent him to bed with the other boys.

"The sky is full tonight," Father Tomaso said.

Dominic turned to look. Father Tomaso's back was to him. His bald head gleamed in the moonlight. And beyond the little crooked window frame, the twinkling of starlight spiraled through the velvety blackness of the night.

Carrying the unlit lantern in his hand, Father Tomaso made his way down the ladder.

As Dominic lay beside the boys in the darkness, he brought his arms across his chest and gently rocked himself back and forth, waiting for the hurt to go away.

"Dominic," Francesco whispered in the darkness. "I promised I would return your kindness the day you took the whip for Antonio, and I meant it. I want you to take Salvatore's ticket and come with us to America. I know he would have wanted it this way. Will you come with us?"

Again, the words of the old man from the museum came back to him. "Open your heart, little one. And all that you need will be yours."

Dominic thought about how he had opened his heart, and how much he had cared about Salvatore, only to find himself hurting now that he was gone. His worst fears had been realized. If he really cared about someone, he would surely lose him. But now that he had opened his heart, he didn't know how to close it.

Dominic's eyes filled with tears as his answer came easily.

"Yes," he whispered, his voice choked by a sob. "I'd like that. I'd like that a lot."

The boys lay silently in the dark. And the only sound that broke the silence was a stifled cry from Francesco as he buried his face in Violetta's soft white fur.

CHAPTER TWENTY-FOUR

THE NEXT MORNING they were awakened early so they could get down to the ship in time for boarding. Signora Giasullo had draped the front doorway in black silk, marking a death in the house. The new Bishop, just transferred from Milan, had seen the doorway on his morning stroll, and though it was not normally done, he stopped in to inquire about the deceased. He and Father Tomaso prayed together for Salvatore's soul.

Meanwhile, the boys had gathered under the arbor for their breakfast.

"The Bishop does us the greatest honor in paying a visit," Dominic heard Signora Giasullo whisper to her husband as she laid the table with sweet cakes and fruit.

Sitting there in the soft morning light, Dominic felt as if they had woken from a bad dream. If he closed his eyes, he could pretend that it was yesterday. He listened to the bees buzzing overhead, just as they had done the day before. The birds were singing their familiar songs and the sun was as warm and comforting as it had been yesterday morning. It was almost as if everything was the same.

But Dominic knew that inside the house something was very different. It was there, in the little sitting room, that the still, lifeless body of Salvatore lay waiting for burial. The women had washed him and combed his hair.

Dominic and Francesco had taken Antonio in to see him, but Antonio was so upset that he had run from the room crying. He just couldn't believe that his brother would never wake up again.

Even now, after they had finally settled him down under the arbor, Antonio kept looking back toward the house. Dominic knew that he was waiting for Salvatore to come walking through the doorway. Dominic himself almost expected to hear that familiar laugh and the excited talk about roping buffalo and eating linguini under the stars. Even Violetta seemed inconsolable, for she had gone under the table and would not come out.

Father Tomaso and the Bishop joined the others at the table. Dominic watched as the Bishop dusted his chair with a handkerchief he had pulled from his sleeve before sitting down. Taking the utmost care, the Bishop placed his fine silk hat on the bench beside him.

"Such a fine hat, your Lordship," Signora Giasullo commented.

"*Grazie,* Signora, thank you," the Bishop replied with a satisfied smile.

With a haughty sniff he surveyed the boys and brought his handkerchief to his nose as if he had smelled something bad. In a strained voice, he began to speak about the salvation of Salvatore's soul. Francesco sat grim-faced, while Antonio dipped his finger into a dish of jam. The Bishop frowned.

This was followed by a soft burp from under the table. Upon hearing this, the Bishop raised his eyebrows, and the boys stifled their giggles. Signora Giasullo quickly changed the subject to church steeples. Grateful for the diversion, the grown-ups all turned in their seats to look at a steeple in the distance.

It was then that Dominic heard a familiar nibbling sound, and noticed that the Bishop's hat was missing from the bench. He quickly kicked Francesco, who slipped under the table to retrieve the silk hat, which he quietly returned to the bench.

Father Tomaso was anxious to leave for the ship and the boys were just as anxious to leave before the Bishop discovered the remains of his hat. After a rushed good-bye, they were on their way. And as they hurried along the cobblestone streets toward the dock, Dominic heard a faint cry coming from under the arbor that sounded like, "My hat! My hat!"

Francesco had tied a rope around Violetta's neck to keep her safe as she trotted along beside him. All along the street people talked excitedly about America and the ship, the *New Amsterdam*.

Dominic smiled at the sound of it. America. He realized for the first time since he had come how much he missed his own country, and he was suddenly overwhelmed by homesickness. As much as he had loved the countryside of Avaletto and the friendship he had found, he longed to see his familiar streets of Brooklyn.

But as happy as he had been about going back to America, he couldn't help but feel the sadness that hung over the group now — the sadness of leaving Salvatore behind, the sadness of Salvatore's dream of going to America that could never come to be.

On reaching the pier, Dominic discovered that theirs was not the only difficult departure. Everywhere people cried and shouted good-byes. Old women wrung their hands and grown men wailed like babies. Dominic remembered the ranger back at the museum saying that Ellis Island was known as "The Island of Hope" and also as "The Island of Tears."

Now he saw how the tears could start even before the immigrants left their homelands. Slowly they made their way past the many little stalls selling clothes, baskets, boxes, and anything that travelers might need for their journey across the ocean.

They waited with Father Tomaso in one long line and then another, nervously eyeing the crowd. If the *padrone's* men had gone up north to look for them, they had nothing to worry about. But if they had changed their minds and headed south, Francesco would be in grave danger.

After what seemed like hours, Father Tomaso finally handed their tickets to an agent, along with their papers. Dominic smiled at Antonio, who squeezed his hand.

As the agent inspected their papers, Violetta tried to eat his shoelaces.

"This is as far as the animal goes," the agent ordered in a gruff voice, shifting his foot from her reach.

"But she meant no harm," Francesco tried to explain.

"No animals on board," the agent snapped.

"But she's with me," Francesco told him.

"Makes no difference," he replied. "No animals allowed."

"She wouldn't know how to get along without me," Francesco pleaded. "We've never been apart, not one night. She wouldn't sleep or eat without me. Who could love her the way I do?"

The shipping agent shrugged.

"You don't understand," Father Tomaso insisted, taking the agent's arm. "The boy has a ticket for America, and she belongs to him. Surely he'd be allowed to take her with him? She's a very well-behaved goat."

The agent shook his head. "Sorry, Father. Passengers are not allowed to take animals. If they allowed animals, there would be no room for people. It's a big boat, but it isn't an ark."

"Ah, such nonsense. One small goat, who would care?" Father Tomaso grumbled as he waved his hand in the air. Then he turned to Francesco, whose face froze when he heard the agent's words:

"Move forward now, and leave the goat behind."

CHAPTER
TWENTY-FIVE

DOMINIC WATCHED as Francesco's hand clutched the rope tighter.

"Give me the rope," Father Tomaso said, placing his hand on Francesco's. "I know how difficult this is for you, but . . ."

"I can't, Father. I can't," Francesco cried, kneeling down beside Violetta.

Violetta moved close to him and tenderly licked his cheek as though she knew what was about to happen.

"Move forward, please," an agent's voice commanded.

The man behind Francesco moved forward, nearly knocking him over.

"My son, give her to me," Father Tomaso whispered. "I will take good care of her. I won't let her out of my sight. I promise you." Gently he took the rope out of his hand. But Francesco hugged Violetta to him, clinging to her for dear life. Violetta's eyes had widened with terror.

"Francesco, I'm surprised at you," Father Tomaso said sternly, punctuating each sentence with a flick of his wrist. "You are the head of your family. Is this how you will act in America? You must set an example for Antonio. You must be brave."

Francesco let go of Violetta, but he didn't take his eyes off her. Finally he stood up. "I'm sorry, Father," he said. "It's just that . . . I shall probably never see her again."

"I know, I know, my son," the priest whispered. "You probably never will see her again." He took all three boys in his arms at once, and, teary-eyed, he gave them one last, loving hug. Then he gave the rope a gentle tug. Violetta followed, looking back at Francesco with a questioning look.

Francesco stared helplessly after her as Dominic grabbed him by the arm, and they made their way up the gangplank. Francesco was frantic to have one last look at Violetta. It was all Dominic could do to hold him back. They searched the crowd below, through the blur of bodies, boxes, and baskets. Francesco was the first to spot her, although she couldn't see him. He watched as her frightened eyes searched through the crowd, looking from one person to the next.

"I'm sorry," Francesco whispered. "I'm so sorry."

He tried to smile through his tears. "Let her sleep near you at night, Father," he yelled into the roar of the crowd. "And don't let her eat bad weeds, and be sure to rub her nose each morning, she likes that, and . . ." Suddenly his voice was drowned out by the deafening sound of the ship's whistle.

The line surged forward, and Antonio clung to Francesco as they were carried along by the wave of people.

The loud whistle of the ship blew again and everyone turned to look back at the docks and wave good-bye to their loved ones. With tears streaming down his face, Francesco stumbled forward, searching in the sea of faces on the wharf.

But by now, Father Tomaso and Violetta had blended into the mass of bodies. People shouted and called out to one another. Their voices all blurred into one loud roar that echoed in Dominic's ears.

"*Arrivederci,* good-bye, my sweet," he saw Francesco mouth the words. "*Arrivederci,* Avaletto, *Arrivederci . . .*"

Dominic's eyes wandered over the crowd, and then beyond them to the hills that rose up from the city. He remembered his first look at Avaletto, the sounds of the birds and the bells, the gentle curves of the trees, the bittersweet smell of lemons.

He thought of the five of them there, Francesco, Salvatore, Antonio, Violetta, and himself. He remembered them talking, laughing, and singing. He recalled the happy times they spent together on those sunny hills.

"Good-bye, Avaletto," Dominic whispered, and as he did, he heard the hushed whispers of hundreds of good-byes all around him.

CHAPTER
TWENTY-SIX

"ALL STEERAGE PASSENGERS, down these stairs!" a voice barked.

Dominic and Antonio were quick to follow the harsh command, while Francesco seemed to be in a daze. Together they found themselves in a crush of people, boxes, and baskets. A man with a thick mustache groaned as he heaved a heavy bundle onto his back that nearly knocked Antonio over. A baby wailed in Dominic's ear as an old woman leaned beside him, breathless under the burden of her parcels. Everyone pushed forward.

"At the bottom of the stairwell, men and boys to the right, women and girls to the left, families to the far end," came the second command.

"Maybe it's better that we're down here," a woman in front of them said. "At least this way we won't feel the cold night air off the sea and it will be drier."

"What does it matter where we have to stay,"

the man beside her answered. "As long as we get to America."

"Yes, finally, we're going to America," voices called out excitedly behind them.

"Going to America," Dominic repeated the words with a smile. He couldn't wait to show Francesco and Antonio his homeland. He couldn't wait to show them the streets he knew, and let them taste the food he liked. He imagined them all sharing a double fries and a couple of burgers. He wanted to do everything with them: watch television, trade baseball cards, and play hockey on the street.

"Do they really have electric lights in all of the buildings?" he heard a voice break into his day-dream.

"Of course they do," someone answered. "It *is* 1908. And it *is* America."

"1908?" Dominic whispered under his breath. It wasn't going to be his America that they were sailing to. It wouldn't be as he remembered at all. *What would it be like? What was ahead of them?* he wondered.

What was ahead of them now was a stairwell, and as they made their way down into the dark, cavernous room, the crowd grew quiet.

We're never going to fit in here, Dominic thought as he looked at the black iron framework that di-vided the hundreds of narrow bunks. Each section had three tiers rising from a bare wooden floor. Thin, straw-filled mattresses covered each bunk. There were no pillows. Some bunks had thin, dirty blankets, but many did not. A bucket serving as a chamber pot was placed near every tier.

The boys found a set of bunks they could share with Francesco. Antonio took the bottom bunk, and Dominic climbed up to the top. When Antonio complained that he was hungry, Francesco gave him a piece of bread that he had saved from the night before.

The other bunks had filled up by this time, and there was a loud echo of voices as people tried to make themselves comfortable.

Dominic laid his head back on the rim of the thin mattress and closed his eyes. As eager as he was to explore the ship, he couldn't help but give in to the exhaustion he was feeling. But the moment he leaned back, his eyes popped open! "Ugh, what stinks?" he groaned.

"It's the straw in the mattress," a man in a bunk beside him answered. "When it gets old and wet it begins to rot. Try not to think about it. We'll be in America soon."

But "soon" stretched out for days and the stink of the moldy mattress was replaced with far worse smells. Almost everyone had brought food with them, and what was not immediately eaten had begun to spoil. The heat of so many bodies cramped together in such tight quarters, with no ventilation, gave way to such an awful stench that by the third day the boys were forced to find relief on the open deck.

Although the air was clean, with a fresh breeze blowing off the ocean, it was also cold and damp. After they inspected as much of the deck as they could, climbing over great coils of rope and ducking under long lengths of pipe, they looked up at the well-dressed passengers strolling on the first- and second-class decks. Once, as they were staring up, a woman threw down an orange to them.

But unlike those first-class passengers dressed in fur coats and heavy wool sweaters, Dominic and the others only had the shirts on their backs to keep off the sea's clammy breath. So they soon discovered that they could keep warm if they pressed against the ship's giant smokestacks. Huddled together there with a half dozen other boys, they traded stories about their dreams of living in America.

They talked about how Francesco and Antonio would live in New Jersey, while Dominic lived in New York. They hoped that one day they would all live together. Francesco grew quiet whenever they mentioned animals, so Dominic tried not to talk about the pets he hoped they could one day have. He knew how much Francesco was missing Violetta.

Dominic hated to think of having to leave them, but he was glad at least that he was returning to New York. He promised to save up his money and come and visit them every chance he got.

But these conversations would come to a sudden end when the weather turned bad and they entered choppy waters. With little warning, the ship would suddenly lurch up into the air on the crest of a billowing wave and then come crashing down on the water's surface. Soaked from the spray and terrified of being tossed overboard in the heavy gales, they would all scramble back to the safety of the steerage dormitories.

On one such day, after returning from the smokestacks, Dominic found himself covered in a film of black grime. Unaccustomed to such filth, he suggested they clean up at the washrooms.

"There are only two rooms for this," Francesco said limply, hanging over his bunk. "And look around you. There are hundreds of us. The lines are so long, why bother? We can wash when we get to America."

"But this is disgusting!" cried Dominic. "I can't stay this dirty until then. Besides, I thought you wanted to look good for America."

"I do, but for now I am feeling too sick to

think of dirt. Everything seems to be moving. Maybe the dirt will move off me as well."

"Well, *I* can't stay like this," Dominic announced, climbing down from his bunk. "I'm going to try one of the washrooms." As he walked on the sticky, splintery floors, he thought about his old sneakers and how much he missed them. After waiting in line for what seemed like hours, he was finally able to move past the wooden partition of what was called "the washroom."

"A bathroom, at last!" Dominic muttered, stepping forward.

"Ugh!" he gasped, covering his nose with his hand to keep from breathing in the horrible stench. The sight that met his eyes was unlike the worst washroom he'd ever been in. The bare wooden floor was sticky with waste, covered only by a thin layer of dirty sand that clung to his bare feet. There were no sinks, no towels, no toilets, and no toilet paper. There were only buckets—wooden buckets filled with salt water to wash in, sitting beside buckets filled to the brim with urine, waste, and vomit. If he hadn't felt sick before he entered the washroom, Dominic certainly did when he left it.

CHAPTER
TWENTY-SEVEN

WHEN HE RETURNED to the bunks, Dominic found Francesco and Antonio talking about what they wanted to be when they grew up.

"When I grow up in America I want to be a very fat man," Antonio said, puffing out his cheeks.

"That's funny," Dominic told him. "Most people don't want to grow up to be fat."

"If I am fat," Antonio explained. "I can live for a long time without food, and my stomach won't hurt, and I'll never be hungry."

"I think even fat people get hungry," Dominic told him.

"When I grow up in America, I will have a big house and a big family," Francesco declared. "And my first-born son will be named Salvatore."

They all grew quiet at the mention of Salvatore.

After the fifth day their conversations turned

from what things they would buy for each other to what kinds of foods they would eat.

For their meals now consisted of the hard biscuits and smelly gray soup that the crew served from big wooden tubs. By the second week, even the drinking water that the ship provided tasted so bad that many people refused to drink it.

"I can smell tobacco in it," Francesco said, making a face as he took a drink. "And I can taste it, too. They must have reused the cask."

Dominic winced as he spit out the foul-tasting liquid. "I think we're getting sick from this water. Our stomach cramps started right after we drank it."

He thought of Salvatore and his stomach pains. Nervously he remembered how quickly his life had ebbed away. Would it be the same for them? Once again, the old man's words came back to him:

"Your courage is there, right alongside of your fear."

Was there enough courage there to see him through this nightmare? As afraid as he was, he also began to feel angry.

"Why doesn't someone complain?" he muttered. "They shouldn't treat us like animals."

"Complain?" Francesco repeated from the bottom bunk. "Who to? The shipping company? And what do you suppose they would do? They'd put us off at the next port, or maybe they wouldn't even wait. Maybe they'd just open the hatch and give a good shove. Do you see how some of the sailors treat us? To them we are no better than dogs. No, it's not wise to complain. We need to get to America, and if that means we must drink dirty water, then that's what we'll do."

"I just hope we don't die before we get there," Dominic moaned, clutching his cramping stomach. His eyes began to wander about the room, and he looked from bunk to bunk at his fellow passengers. He could read the exhaustion on their faces, the weariness in their slack jaws. He could see the sickly green tint to their complexions, the white of their knuckles as they clutched the iron bars of their berths. He could hear the moans and groans, the prayers and lamentations that accompanied each loud creak of the ship's wooden walls. But try as he might he couldn't hear anger, the anger that he would have expected to accompany such miserable conditions.

No one was demanding his money back! No one was threatening to sue the shipping company. They seemed to accept the misery as part of their payment to reach America. He tried closing his eyes, but that only made the continual rocking seem worse and the stench grow stronger. This lasted for the remainder of the trip, until the days and nights began to run into each other and he had lost all track of time.

And then, on the fifteenth day, word came down to them that land had been sighted. Hoots and cheers filled the air as the exciting news was passed from bunk to bunk. High spirits spread through the ship like wildfire. People kissed, hugged, laughed, and cried. They had spotted land! American land!

With trembling hands, Francesco shook Antonio awake.

"America!" Antonio croaked, rubbing the sleep from his eyes. "Are we really going to see America?"

"Yes, Antonio," Francesco laughed as he pulled out two shirts from his cloth pack. "And we are going to look our best for our new country."

Francesco and Antonio changed into their clean shirts. Then Francesco reached into the sack and pulled out the remaining one. Everyone grew quiet at the sight of it. Dominic looked down at the small worn shirt in Francesco's hands and he knew what the others were thinking.

He knew they were thinking of Salvatore and how he should be here, to wear the shirt, and to see America.

"Go on," Francesco said, holding the shirt out to Dominic. "Put it on. Salvatore would have wanted you to wear it."

Dominic quickly undid the little wooden buttons. He slipped his arms into the sleeves. He knew that if he were to wear such a threadbare garment in his own time, kids would really make fun of him. But as he looked down at the stained shirt now and tried to smooth out the wrinkles with his dirty hands, Dominic felt as if he had never worn anything finer.

CHAPTER
TWENTY-EIGHT

THERE WERE OVER a thousand passengers aboard the *New Amsterdam*, and most of them clamored onto the decks, anxious to get a first glimpse of their new country. Dominic and the others had to wait in a long line by the stairwell. When they were finally able to make their way up the steps, they had to squeeze their way to the deck's railing.

An awed hush fell over the crowd as they sailed into the Hudson Bay and caught their first glimpse of the New York skyline. Many of the passengers gaped over the deck's rails, having never seen a building higher than two stories.

At the sight of the Statue of Liberty, everyone became silent. With her torch held high, her calm strength standing firm against wind and water, she awed everyone, and moved many to tears.

Dominic stared at his favorite statue and felt his own tears welling in his eyes. For he finally understood just how much her welcoming and powerful presence meant to the immigrants who had come so far.

"It's good to see you again, Lady Liberty," he whispered as they sailed past the towering figure.

Staring out at the New York skyline, Dominic couldn't believe his eyes. Everything seemed so short! Where were his old favorites? The Empire State Building and the twin towers were no where to be seen. In fact, most of his favorite buildings were gone. He realized with a shock that this was indeed what New York looked like in 1908!

"It's not New York!" he gasped.

"Sure it is," a man standing beside him said.

"No, not my New York," Dominic whispered under his breath. The realization that he might never see his New York and his world in his own time gripped him with fear.

If Francesco and Antonio were to live in New Jersey, then Dominic would be living alone with yet another strange family in New York. But this would be the New York of 1908. Suddenly he felt the old familiar feelings of loneliness sweeping over him. Only this time they were accompanied with a new fear. How was he to fit in to a new family in such an old time? It had been easy with Francesco and the others, but what if this new family wasn't nice to him? What if they didn't like him? Who could he turn to for help in the New York of 1908?

It took hours for them to disembark onto the Hudson River Pier. Antonio began to get restless, and Francesco and Dominic took turns carrying him on their shoulders.

By the time they reached the pier, everyone was anxious to feel solid ground under their feet once again. No one complained of the long wait for the ferries to arrive, for it was a relief just not to be bobbing up and down on the boat. Dominic watched as thousands of faces passed by, crammed onto the decks of the many steamships and ferries that choked the harbor.

A ferryman called out a command in English. Dominic and the others could not make out his words, but they could see his hands directing them onto the gangplanks. In a crush of baskets, boxes, and suitcases they were all packed onto the ferries for the ride to Ellis Island.

There was another long wait before the ferry's engines started up. As they began to move, Dominic remembered his last ferry ride over to Ellis Island, and how very different it had been. He remembered how much room everyone had aboard the ship. He had actually run on the decks! No one had been dirty or hungry or sick. Everyone had been wearing clean clothes and people had laughed and joked.

No one was laughing now as he stood squeezed between an old grizzled-faced man that smelled of cheese and vomit and a woman carrying a crying baby who smelled every bit as bad. Bundles, boxes, and bodies pressed against him as Dominic struggled to get a breath of fresh air.

When the castle-like facade of Ellis Island came clearly into view, a cheer went up and the air crackled with excitement.

"Such a palace!" Antonio marveled.

"They really do live like kings and queens here!" a woman beside them whispered. A wave of goosebumps rolled across Dominic's arms as he stared at the horse-drawn carriages and carts that lined the docks.

Meanwhile, anxious conversations had sprung up throughout the crowd as the immigrants nervously eyed the imposing buildings on the island.

"The button-hook men are the worst!" Dominic heard a boy behind them say. "They turn your eyelids inside out with their hooks!"

"Why do they do such things?" Antonio asked, turning around.

"That is how they look for disease in the eye. It's part of the *batteria,* what they put you through before you are allowed into the country," came the whispered reply.

Antonio began to rub his eyes fearfully as they followed the crowd off the ferry and into the long line that snaked its way up to Ellis Island's main entrance. Everyone was talking about the battery of inspections that was given to weed out those who were not fit to enter America.

"What if we do not pass the inspections?" Francesco asked nervously.

"Don't worry," Dominic assured him. "Just answer the questions the way the ticket agents told us to and everything will be all right."

The ticket agents, who worked for the shipping companies, had already gone over these questions with their passengers, feeding them the correct answers. For any immigrant not accepted into America was sent back at the shipping company's expense.

But now, standing so close to their dreams, with so much depending on each answer, everyone grew worried.

"What if we make mistakes?" Francesco whispered anxiously. "What if we don't give the right answers? Antonio, don't stick your tongue out like that. You don't want them to think you are an idiot."

"Just don't think about it so much," Dominic said, trying to sound confident.

After waiting for a long time, Dominic and Antonio sat down in the line, too tired to stand any longer. They were under the canopy leading to the building's large doors, leaning against a big pillar. Francesco reached into his pocket and pulled out Salvatore's gold key and chain. He put the chain around his neck. Dominic's heart leaped at the sight of it.

"The key! You have the key!" he cried. Dominic leaned back against the pillar, dumbstruck. With so much happening, he had forgotten to ask about the key.

Francesco lowered his head sadly and placed his hand over the key. Dominic leaned in closer, as Francesco said in a whisper, "I will wear it for you, Salvatore. I shall keep it close to my heart, until my own son can wear it."

CHAPTER
TWENTY-NINE

MEANWHILE ANTONIO had bent down and picked up a small rusty pin.

"Antonio, give me that pin," Francesco demanded. "We don't need you to scratch yourself now!"

Francesco stood beside them and, as he leaned against a pillar, he began to scratch a little picture onto its plaster surface.

"Why do you get to use the pin and I don't?" Antonio complained.

"Because I am older and more careful," Francesco explained.

"What are you drawing?" Antonio demanded, jumping up to get a closer look.

"The most beautiful goat in Italy," Francesco said softly as he continued to draw.

"But you've given her wings," observed Antonio. "Goats don't have wings."

"It's what I wish for her to have," Francesco

whispered. "With wings she could fly to America."

"Come, Dominic," Antonio called. "Come and see Francesco's funny drawing. Come see Violetta with wings."

Dominic looked at the drawing and smiled. "It's good," he said, "but she's not eating anything." Francesco smiled too, and was about to draw something for her to eat, when the line suddenly lurched forward and they found themselves moving through the big doors.

Antonio covered his ears with his hands, for the din of noise in the great hall was deafening. A great swell of sound echoed off the walls and bounced around them as people were talking, laughing, crying, and yelling, all in different languages and all at once.

Dominic's eyes searched the empty walls as they began the climb up the grand staircase. Gone were the photographs, gone were the displays. There were no tourists with cameras, no gift shops, no computer screens. There were just people, lots and lots of people. It was as though all of the photos and displays from the museum had suddenly come to life! Dominic and the others stared wide-eyed at the strange assortment of faces and clothing.

When they had finally reached the first desk and the inspector had looked over their papers, he tried talking to them in English. Dominic was stunned to realize that, hard as he tried, he couldn't remember a single word of the language. It was as though he had never known it!

"*Non parlo inglese,* I don't speak English," Francesco told the inspector. "*Parla italiano?* Do you speak Italian?" Francesco asked the man.

But the man shook his head no and called for an interpreter to help them. Then he pointed to the names on the tickets and spoke again in English, in words the boys could not understand.

The interpreter, who knew English and Italian, translated for them.

"Cantori brothers, go to the next line," he said.

"Cantori?" Dominic whispered. "Why did he say Cantori? How does he know my name?"

"*Mi chiamo* Candiano," Francesco tried to explain to the man. "My name is Candiano. We are the Candiano brothers."

The man took their tickets and showed them where the shipping agent had written their names.

"Antonio Cantori, Salvatore Cantori, and Francesco Cantori," the man read aloud. "Cantori."

"What happened to Candiano?" Francesco asked.

The interpreter shrugged. "The shipping agent wrote it as Cantori. That's your name now."

Dominic stared as chills shot up his spine.

"But that is not our name," Francesco cried.

"Maybe not in Italy," the interpreter explained. "But here, in America, it is. Things are not like they were back in Italy. You have crossed the ocean. You are Americans now."

Francesco thought this over. "Cantori," he whispered, rolling the name over on his tongue. "*Sono americano*, I am an American. I am a Cantori."

"That's my name!" Dominic cried.

"Yes, now it can be your name, too," Francesco agreed.

"No, you don't understand . . ." his voice trailed off to a whisper as he caught sight of the glint of gold peeking out from under Francesco's shirt. It was Salvatore's key. The key that would one day be his own.

"S.C.," Dominic whispered the initials he knew so well under his breath and suddenly he began to understand. If Francesco's name was now Cantori, and if he kept the key to give to his son, and that son gave it to his son, and it eventually came to Dominic, then . . . could that mean . . . that Francesco was Dominic's great-grandfather?

CHAPTER THIRTY

DOMINIC STARED AT FRANCESCO. He could see the resemblance now. Francesco's eyes were the same color and shape as his own. They both loved animals and they had the same laugh. Why hadn't he recognized it before?

My great-grandfather! he thought. He longed to tell Francesco all about it. But he knew that Francesco would think he was crazy or "sick in the head from the earthquake."

Meanwhile Antonio had to go to the bathroom and Francesco was ready to take him outside when the man behind them told them about the indoor toilets.

Dominic was to keep their seats until they returned. But as he watched them walk away, an odd fear suddenly gripped him. Maybe he should go after them, maybe he shouldn't let them out of his sight. Now that he had found them and he knew who they really were, and who he was to them, Dominic wanted them close by.

He waited anxiously for them to return, and when they finally did, Dominic sighed with relief. As they stepped forward in line they heard a woman in front of them talking about the "Italian Aid Society." She pointed to a table that people were crowding around. "They will help you find the people you are to meet," the woman was saying.

Dominic and Francesco looked at the table and then at each other. They both knew that their time together was coming to an end.

"Francesco," Dominic began.

"Yes," Francesco answered.

"I don't know," Dominic fumbled for the right words. He felt suddenly embarrassed, and lowered his eyes to the floor. "It's just that everything is happening so fast," he blurted out. "And soon you'll be off to New Jersey and I might not see you for a while."

Francesco nodded his head as if he understood. Dominic looked up to meet his large, dark eyes, eyes that matched his own.

"I'll never forget you," Dominic whispered. "All of you. And I hope you won't forget me."

"Forget?" Francesco smiled. "Who could forget *famiglia?*"

He reached out and hugged Dominic hard.

And this time, for the first time, Dominic hugged him back.

"What about me?" Antonio squeaked. Dominic grinned and bent down to give him a big hug, too.

"I bet you won't even recognize me the next time you see me, Dominic," Antonio announced.

"No, why not?" Dominic asked.

"Because I am going to eat so much food here in America, that I will look as if . . ."

"As if you are made like a mushroom?" Dominic finished his sentence. The three boys stood silent for a second, and then they all began to laugh as they wrapped their arms around each other in one big hug.

They stood in line for a long, long time, until it had stopped moving altogether. People had begun to sit on their suitcases and bundles. Dominic was glad that the line wasn't moving. They hadn't slept much the night before, and they hadn't eaten in hours. All the excitement of landing had left them exhausted. Dominic and Antonio slumped down against the back of a large basket beside a woman nursing a baby. It felt so good to sit that Dominic decided not to get back up until he had to. He felt his eyes begin to droop.

Dominic watched as Antonio tapped his grimy little fingers over the brightly painted red and yellow flowers on his concertina. The baby in the mother's arms beside them began to fuss, and Antonio offered to play a lullaby to help calm him.

The song was so soothing that Dominic found it hard to keep his eyes open.

"Just a little nap," he mumbled as his head began to fall onto his chest. He thought he heard Francesco call his name over the din of voices, and the soft melody of the concertina. And then he heard nothing at all.

CHAPTER THIRTY-ONE

"WAKE UP, SON," a deep voice called.

"Francesco?" Dominic moaned, his eyes still closed.

Blinking hard, Dominic looked up to see a man in modern clothes staring down at him.

"Now where did you come from?" the man asked in English.

"Where am I?" Dominic cried. "Where's Francesco?" He was shocked to hear himself speak in English.

"You're at the Ellis Island Immigration Museum. I'm one of the rangers here."

"The museum?" Dominic gasped. "Rangers?" He looked down to see his clean T. Rex T-shirt. And there on his chest, hanging from the gold chain, was his lucky key. He clutched it with his trembling fingers. "What year is it?" he whispered.

"I suppose if you hang around long enough in

here," the ranger laughed, "you do sort of forget what year it is."

"No, you don't understand," Dominic tried to explain. "You see, I was here with my class when I fell asleep, and then I woke —"

"I think what happened is you fell asleep and you had yourself quite a dream," the ranger interrupted. "What's your name, kid?"

"Dominic. Dominic Cantori," he sputtered.

"What happened to your shoes?"

Dominic stared down at his bare feet, his clean, unbruised feet.

"I . . . I . . . left them in the closet downstairs," he said.

"Don't worry, we'll pick them up," the ranger told him as he helped him to his feet. Dominic looked around at the softly lit display cases and the modern lighting overhead. He took a deep breath. The air was clean and cool.

"Come on, we'd better get downstairs and give your family a call," the ranger said.

"My family?" Dominic repeated the words aloud.

Before the ranger could stop him, Dominic spun around and reached for the phone where he had first heard Francesco's voice. And as his heart pounded in his chest, he held the receiver to his ear.

CHAPTER
THIRTY-TWO

"I CAME TO AMERICA when I was a boy of eleven years old. . . ." the familiar old voice began.

"Francesco," Dominic whispered into the receiver. "It's me, Dominic!" He held his breath and waited for the reply.

"In Italy we had very little, and yet we had so much. . . ." the voice continued.

"I know, I know. You had Violetta, and Father Tomaso, and your brothers, and me. You had me. You said we were *famiglia*. Remember? Francesco please just say you remember," Dominic pleaded.

"In Italy we had a goat. . . ."

"Come on, kid," the ranger said, trying to take the receiver from his hand. "What do you say we get downstairs now?"

"I just wanted to hear him say that he remembers," Dominic whispered.

Dominic reluctantly put down the phone and followed the ranger through the display rooms, into the hall, past the large photographs hanging on the walls. But he slowed his pace and stared up at the many faces of the newly arrived immigrants in the pictures. He felt an eerie stillness in the cooled air, an unnatural quiet, as the faces looked back at him, frozen in time.

"They were all talking," Dominic whispered. "I heard their voices. I heard the babies crying and the people talking. They were laughing and shouting and alive. They were all alive. . . ."

The ranger began to head back toward the escalator when Dominic stopped suddenly.

"Wait," he said, lifting his T-shirt. "On my back. Do you see the marks on my back?"

The ranger leaned over to look at his back. "No, I don't see any marks there."

"Maybe I did dream it," Dominic said, lowering his shirt as they continued walking down the hall. "It's just that they all seemed so real. They were all wearing old-fashioned clothes like the ones in those displays," he said, pointing to a glass case.

The ranger just shook his head. "Come on," he said, gently taking Dominic's arm. They were heading through a doorway when Dominic broke free and ran off in the other direction. As the ranger called for him to stop, Dominic made a dash for the escalator and raced up the steps to the third floor.

He hurried from room to room, from one display to the next. Was it all a dream? Or had it really happened? He had to find something that would tell him for sure.

He stopped finally to catch his breath and as he leaned against another large glass display case, he looked up to see the words in the case, "Immigrant Graffiti." Dominic pressed his face to the glass and peered into the case.

"Okay, kid, I'm out of patience," a voice suddenly called as the ranger came up behind him and grabbed his arm. "This time we're going downstairs."

But Dominic didn't answer. He couldn't answer, for he was speechless. When his voice finally returned, he could think of only one word to say.

"Violetta," he whispered, placing his trembling fingers on the glass. For there in the case before him was a cracked piece of plaster on which the delicate outline of a little goat had been scratched. And from the goat's shoulders sprouted two graceful wings.

CHAPTER THIRTY-THREE

THREE WEEKS LATER Dominic sat in Dave Santos's office at the child welfare department.

"I know it hasn't been easy for you these last few years," Dave said. "I know you've had some bad breaks. I'm sorry about this last family deciding to move to California. But I've been looking, and I think I found the right one this time.

"They're nice people, Dominic. They have a big house with a yard, and two other boys live with them. And this is the best part. The kids were foster kids that they've adopted! They want a family. And they are willing to adopt an older child. It won't be like some of those other homes, where you were there on a temporary basis. If you can just bear with us, and try one more time, this could be the one. Now let me find their file."

As Dave shuffled through a pile of papers on

his desk, Dominic thought about his modern American dream family. Then he thought about his *famiglia* in Italy. How would he ever find a family he could love as much as he'd loved them? He closed his eyes as their voices filled his ears. He could hear Francesco whispering to Violetta. He could hear Salvatore dreaming aloud about cowboys, and Antonio singing along to the gentle notes from his concertina.

"So, what do you say, Dominic?" Dave asked, looking up from his file. "Are you ready to try another one? Can I tell them we'll meet with them tomorrow morning?"

Dominic opened his eyes. "I'm ready," he said.

"Oh, and by the way," Dave added. "The father is a veterinarian, so the kids have lots of pets."

Dominic's eyebrows shot up. "What kind of pets?" he asked.

"Oh, let me see. There were dogs, a cat, a snake, an iguana, a parrot, and . . ."

"A goat?" Dominic asked.

"A goat?"

Dominic grinned. "They make the best pets," he said.

"I don't know about goats." Dave laughed. "We'll have to wait and see. You'll continue to stay with the Jensens until they're ready to move out to California next week. Or, if we can settle on this family tomorrow, you could be moved in by Friday."

Later that night as he lay in the darkness of his bedroom at the Jensens' house, Dominic couldn't stop thinking about his adventure. Had he really gone to Italy? Had he really met his family? Was Francesco really his great-grandfather? Somehow, he was sure it was all true.

Dominic reached for the golden key around his neck. He rubbed his fingers over the worn initials S.C. Then he thought about the boy who first found that key so long ago in that far-off place, and how he had wished for it to unlock some buried treasure.

Outside Dominic's window the traffic sped by while the noise from the TV echoed off the walls in the room beside him. A man and a woman shouted in the apartment over his head. And yet the only sound that Dominic heard was the song of a small concertina as it accompanied the rustlings of the olive leaves in the wind.

Maybe the key had unlocked a treasure after all, he thought. For now he understood how he had always been and would always be a part of a family. And he could *never* lose those he loved, not completely. Francesco and the others would be part of who he was for the rest of his life.

"The rest of my life," Dominic whispered aloud.

As Dominic thought about the new people he'd be meeting tomorrow, the words of his great-grandfather — Francesco Cantori — drifted back to him, lulling him to sleep:

"Open your heart, little one," he heard the old man tell him. "And all that you need shall be yours."

Author's father *(right)* and uncle *(left)*
in San Marco Square, Venice, Italy, 1934

AUTHOR'S NOTE

BETWEEN 1880 AND 1914 nearly three million Italians came to America to find a new home. Eighty percent of them came from the Mezzogiorno (the region south of Rome) and from the island of Sicily. In the hills just northeast of Naples, in that same region, is the village of Avellino, on which I based the fictitious town of Avaletto. This is where my grandparents were born and lived until they were ready to begin families of their own.

The lesson I learned from my parents and they from theirs is that *famiglia,* family, is all important. When a family's survival is in jeopardy, no sacrifice is too great.

As much as the Italians loved their homeland, they were experiencing great deprivations at the end of the nineteenth century, caused in part by earthquakes and blights that decimated the vineyards and fruit trees. Thousands of people were left penniless and at the mercy of the *padroni,* the landlords, who treated their workers no better than slaves. Life was hard and there was little hope of betterment. When news arrived from across the ocean that America could offer freedom and a better life, both of my grandfathers (who had not yet met at the time), joined the millions of

Italians, who made the difficult decision to leave for America. More than three quarters of the emigrants leaving Italy at this time were men.

Like most of their countrymen, neither of my grandfathers spoke any English when they arrived at Ellis Island, but they had a desire to learn and to prosper. On their arrival in America, they found that modernization and industrialization were in full swing. There was a great demand for unskilled labor, and they were able and willing to fill this demand.

My father's father, Giovanni Pirozzi, took his first job in a cigar factory in New Jersey. He went on to deliver cigars to upstate New York with a horse and wagon. My grandfather learned so much about the business of transportation that he formed his own company, which later became a prosperous trucking firm. My grandmother came to America with her family as a young girl. After she married my grandfather, they had four sons together.

My mother's father, Francesco Giasullo, took a job building the subways in New York City. After a few years he returned to Italy to find a wife and to bring her back with him to live in New York City's Little Italy. But my grandmother was not happy living in the city. She missed the fresh air and the trees. She missed the flowers in her garden.

Eventually she and my grandfather saved

enough money to buy farm land in New Jersey. There my grandfather grew grapes for wine and made cheese to sell. My grandmother planted cherry trees and roses and had seven children on that farm. She died suddenly when my mother was only three years old. It seems my grandmother had a sudden case of appendicitis caused by the cherry pits she had swallowed. (I was thinking of her when I wrote about Salvatore's death, but she was not swallowing the pits to fill an empty stomach. Although if she had stayed in Italy, that may have been reason for doing so.)

While my grandparents' names were not changed upon entering America, as the names of the Candiano brothers and many other immigrants had been, my mother and her sisters and brothers had their names changed when they entered public school! The officials at the school thought their name, Giasullo, would be too difficult to pronounce, and they suggested changing it to Gesnee, which they thought sounded more American. The school also suggested that my uncle Crescenzo change his name to Jack.

Today my grandparents' farm is gone, transformed into a housing development. Gone are the roses and the fruit trees; gone is the little grape arbor out back along with the red barn and the old willow tree that stood beside it. Gone, too, are the voices of those young parents who came so far and struggled so much to make a better life for their children.

And what remains? The children and grandchildren and great-grandchildren and all the children to come. What remains is *famiglia*.

Italian Americans today still carry on the traditions inherited from their families across the ocean. The preparation and enjoyment of fresh food was and is as important to Italians as the air they breathe.

You cannot walk into my mother's house without her offering you food of some sort. Her pizza dough sits rising in a big bowl on the stove, while she stands at the counter chopping herbs. A patch of basil grows at her kitchen door and her little house is circled with hollyhocks and roses.

As I walk to the post office in my village of Martins Creek, Pennsylvania, a village settled by many Italian stone workers, I pass by carefully tended gardens with tomato plants reaching for the sky and flowers spilling over window boxes.

The same warmth and friendliness that Dominic experienced when meeting the Candiano brothers in Avaletto is still present in Italian American communities today.

Last year, I stopped at "Rome's" gas station in Martins Creek and I found a neighbor grilling sausage and peppers in the parking lot! He explained that every year, when the first peppers come up in his garden, he likes to set up his grill so he can share his good fortune.

If you were to visit Italy today, you would see much that has remained unchanged for centuries, and much that has changed. While the ringing of church bells can still be heard, the sound of donkey bells has all but vanished. The little cobblestone streets are now more often than not clogged with small cars and motorbikes.

Italy's natural beauty — the golden light falling on the ancient stone buildings, the blue of the sea, the sweeping greens of the olive and cypress trees — still remains as it has for hundreds of years. As a seventeenth-century visitor to Italy once remarked on the landscape, "Here the beautie of all the world is gathered as it were into a bundle." Unfortunately, poor ecological regulations have caused many problems in the country. On a recent visit to the city of Milan I saw people wearing gas masks as they walked to work — the smog from the city's traffic was so threatening!

But in that same city I was able to visit one of the world's most beautiful cathedrals, The Duomo, which dates back to the year 1386. I was also able to view the drawings for a helicopter that Leonardo da Vinci had made in that city over five hundred years ago, as well as his magnificently painted fresco, *The Last Supper,* in the church of Santa Maria delle Grazie. That evening, at the city's most famous opera house, La Scala, there was a performance that left the audience in tears of joy.

Many aspects of our daily lives in America today — our churches, our music, our art, and many of our favorite foods — can be traced to Italian influences. From the invention of the piano, to the creation of pizza and ice cream, Italy's legacy lives on!

Millions of immigrants have crossed the ocean as Dominic and the Candiano brothers did. With their courage and spirit they have all enriched their adopted country. And while we study our differences and appreciate our many unique qualities, let us not forget that we are all Americans, all *famiglia*.

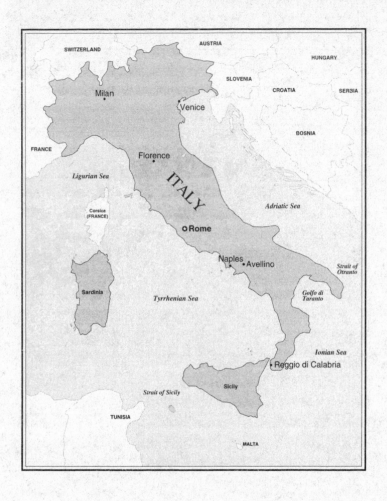

GLOSSARY

PRONUNCIATION GUIDE FOR NAMES AND PLACES

BIBLIOGRAPHY

Baroni, Arturo. *Italians First*. Kent, England: Renaissance Books, 1994.

Costantino, Mario and Lawrence Gambella. *The Italian Way.* Chicago: Passport Books, 1996.

Delle Donne, Vincenzo, ed. *Naples (Insights Guides)*. New York: Houghton Mifflin, 1993.

Fisher, Leonard. *Ellis Island*. New York: Holiday House Inc., 1986.

Harrison, Barbara Grizzuti. *Italian Days.* New York: Weidenfeld and Nicolson, 1989.

Levine, Ellen. *If Your Name Was Changed at Ellis Island*. New York: Scholastic Inc., 1993.

Mangione, Jerre and Ben Morreale. *La Storia: Five Centuries of the Italian American Experience.* New York: HarperCollins, 1992.

Morrison, Joan and Charlotte Fox Zabusky. *American Mosaic.* Pittsburgh and London: University of Pittsburgh Press, 1980.

Tifft, Wilton S. *Ellis Island*. Chicago: Contemporary Books, 1990.

Weldon, Owen. *Italy: A Culinary Journey.* San Francisco: Collins Publishers, 1991.